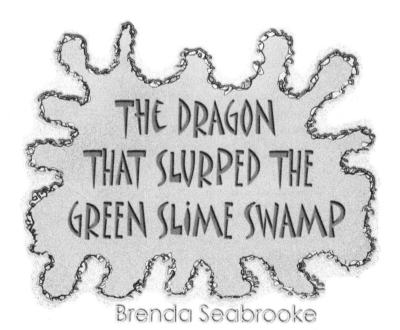

THE DRAGON THAT SLURPED THE GREEN SLIME SWAMP

Brenda Seabrooke

ISBN-13: 978-1523492343
ISBN-10: 1523492341

Chapter 1

Alastair McKnight wadded a mostly clean T-shirt, underwear and pajama bottoms together and stuffed them into the duffle bag on his bed. Shorts, a softball and an armload of comics followed. Then he took the comics out and added them to an already bulging backpack. He might want them on the way. You never knew when you needed to read a comic book.

Spike his baby blue dragon watched with interest from the top of the dresser.

"Are you packed yet, Alastair?" his mom called. "Uncle George will be here any minute."

Alastair tossed in more tee shirts, a ball glove and bat and one bedroom shoe. He couldn't find its mate so what good was one? He dropped it on the floor and kicked it under his bed. That left more room for his scientific equipment.

"*Mewlp*," Spike said from the dresser.

Alastair didn't know how Spike got up there. Baby blue dragons can't jump high and Spike didn't have any signs of wings. Uncle George said he might be a terrestrial dragon. That meant land dragon, not a flying one but they would have to wait and see. Now Spike slid down the side of the dresser and climbed up Alastair's green bedspread. He hopped on top of the ball glove and sat beaming his curly dragon smile at Alastair.

Alastair sighed. This wasn't going to be easy. "I'm sorry, Spike. You can't go this time." Alastair picked Spike up and put him on the floor. He pushed Spike's toy car with his foot and sent it into the middle of the room. That usually distracted Spike. Baby blue dragons can hardly ever resist things with wheels.

Except today.

Spike ignored the car and climbed up the bed again. He stomped across clothes and toys and crawled into the duffle bag all the while muttering dragon noises to himself. *Grummmpfff. Groiwffffwyl. Grouwmmmmmp.* He turned around three times and curled up in the ball glove.

"Sorry, little guy. I really am but you can't go this time. I explained it all to you already."

Spike looked at him as if he had never seen Alastair before.

"You know Josh and I are going to the Green Slime Swamp with Uncle George. We're going to look for the Lizard Man."

Spike didn't seem to remember. Alastair lifted him out of the glove and set him on the floor. He threw a pair of jeans and some mostly clean socks into the bag. The room got quiet. No dragon noises. Not little car noises. Alastair looked down.

Spike stood on all four feet where Alastair had deposited him. He stared up at Alastair with his round dragon eyes under curly dragon eyelashes. A fat dragon tear rolled down his cheek and plopped onto a sock.

"I'm sorry, fella. There's just no place for a baby blue dragon on a scientific expedition."

Spike's eyes grew rounder and bigger and more pitiful. A waterfall of dragon tears spilled down his cheeks. They splashed in a little pool around the now-soaked sock.

Alastair didn't know what to do. He had worked hard all year to keep his grades up so he and his best friend Josh could go on this trip with Uncle George, a scientist at the Photon Institute. Josh had kept his grades up, too. The thought of a trip had kept them going through the fourth grade with the toughest teacher in Hilliard Middle School, Ms. Cassowary. This trip was a dream come true. Alastair had earned his way writing all those papers for Ms. Cassowary, but how could he leave his pet dragon? Spike would be lost without Alastair. No one to play with or take him for walks in his Teagle suit.

"It won't be for long, Spike. I'll be back before you know I'm gone almost."

Not true. Alastair knew it and Spike knew it.

Spike uttered a hiccuppy sob. More tears gushed from his little round eyes and plopped into the pool.

Alastair remembered what had happened when he had gone back to school last September. The dragon thought he had done something wrong and Alastair didn't love him anymore. He had stopped eating. Alastair had to convince Spike he was a very loved dragon and coax him to eat again.

Uncle George said they might be gone for two weeks or even more. What if Spike decided Alastair had abandoned him again? He wouldn't be here to reassure his pet dragon he was still loved and hadn't been abandoned. Spike was a growing dragon and needed his food. He might starve if he stopped eating, even for a week.

Mom had promised to take extra special care of Spike but she worked at the library. Dad was at his office all day. His sister Claudia was busy with her friends and going to cheerleader camp. Nobody would be around to coax Spike to eat again.

Spike was a small dragon. He wouldn't take up much room. Nobody would even know Alastair had brought him along. Not even Josh.

Without another thought, Alastair crammed the rest of his clothes and things into the duffle bag. He could sort them out later. He patted the jumble of clothes. Spike stopped in mid-sniff and looked up at Alastair with hopeful little eyes.

"Hop in, little guy, and be really quiet."

Still snuffling, Spike climbed up on the bed and packed himself in the bag. He smiled and settled himself soggily in the duffle.

Now he was a happy dragon.

Now Alastair wouldn't have to worry about Spike being sad and not eating.

Now Alastair was thinking ahead like Mom and Dad were always telling him.

Problem solved!

He wouldn't tell his parents or Uncle George. They would say it was too risky to expose Spike to dragonappers again. Alastair was confident he could take care of Spike. He had been taking care of him since finding the baby dragon in the petunia bed last summer.

He had thwarted dragonappers.

He knew more about dragons than anybody in the whole world. He was the world expert on baby blue dragons. Uncle George said so.

He knew what was best for his dragon.

What could possibly go wrong?

Chapter 2

Spike snuggled into the baseball glove. Alastair glanced one more time around his room. What was he forgetting?

Dragon food.

He loped to the kitchen where Claudia sat at the table slurping her breakfast cereal. Her face was smeared with white Goooop. She slept in the stuff and wore it at home when nobody but family was around to see her. She looked like a clown, an unfunny one. She claimed the stuff kept her zit-free. Claudia was in junior high. That's where you learn about zit-control and other stuff. Alastair thought Claudia was a giant zit. She felt the same way about him.

He looked in the fridge while she fished dried strawberries out of the bowl. She hated strawberries. Maybe she wouldn't notice what he was up to. He took a bag of carrots out of the produce drawer. He wanted to take celery too, but that might be noticed. He slid a stick in the carrot bag anyway.

"You're taking CARROTS?" Claudia's voice rose on the last word into a kind of screech. A dried strawberry flew across the room.

"Hey—watchit." Alastair ducked.

Another strawberry sailed by his ear. "When did you start eating carrots?"

Alastair thought fast. "Eye food. Ms. Cassowary said carrots are good for your eyes. They will help us see the Lizard Man better at night."

Claudia snorted. "Like there really is such a thing."

"Some people don't think there are any dragons around either but we know different, don't we?"

That shut her up, but not for long.

"Why don't people see this Lizard Man?"

"People have seen him," Alastair said. "We just have to prove it. That's why we're going on this expedition."

"Alastair, hurry up. Uncle George is here," Mom called from the carport.

He grabbed a bag of sunflower seeds and ran to his room. These and the carrots would keep Spike from starving until he could get to a store to buy more dragon food. He threw Spike's Teagle disguise suit into the backpack with the food.

Alastair had a feeling he was forgetting something. He went over his mental list: comic books, clothes, notebook,

beside his as Josh said in a loud voice, "Hey, what you got in there, your grandma's china?"

Alastair gave him a shove.

Josh shoved back.

"Cool it," Alastair said under his breath.

"What?" Josh said. "Cool what?"

Josh could be so dense.

Claudia wandered out of the kitchen to give Uncle George a hug.

"Sorry you aren't coming, too," he said.

She had washed her face and combed her rats' nest blond hair. Alastair was glad she wasn't coming with them. That was one of the best parts of the trip. Two weeks away from Claudia and her silly mall rat friends.

Alastair hugged his mom and climbed in the back seat of the van. "Come on, Josh."

Josh never liked to be left behind. He jumped in beside Alastair. "Bye, Mrs. McKnight. Bye, Claudia."

"Everybody ready to roll?" Uncle George asked.

"Ready," Alastair and Josh said together.

A funny little gleeping noise came from the back of the van but Uncle George didn't hear it. He closed the doors and slid behind the wheel. Everybody buckled up and he started the engine.

The boys waved through the window as the van rolled into the street and drove past Mr. Hobson's house next door. Mr. Hobson didn't seem to be home. If he had been, Alastair was sure he would be out waving them off, glad to have a vacation from Alastair and Josh and, if he only knew, Spike. (He didn't know Spike was a dragon. He thought the dragon was a dog because Alastair disguised him as a Teagle and said he was a rare breed from China.)

He would not have been as glad as Alastair and Josh were to have a vacation from him. Mr. Hobson thought the two schemed all the time to think of ways to wreck his flowers. They never once even bruised a petal. It was Mr. Hobson and Gruesome, the Whipples's boxer. They were the ones who damaged Mr. Hobson's garden.

The truth was, Alastair had to admit to himself, Spike was responsible for some of the damage to the prize flowers. He was a vegetarian dragon and loved to eat Mr. Hobson's juicy flowers but he wouldn't have eaten them if Gruesome hadn't run into the garden.

Somehow Mr. Hobson's prize flowers always got ruined just before a flower show. It seemed to Alastair that there were flower shows all the time. Like almost every week.

Alastair had kept Spike out of the flowers for a long time now. They were probably all ripe for another flower show so he was really doing Mr. Hobson a favor taking Spike with him. Mr. Hobson would probably appreciate Alastair's thoughtfulness.

If he knew about it.

Which he didn't.

Mr. Hobson's flowers were safe now for the next two weeks. Alastair was sure he was had done the right thing bringing Spike along. The more he thought about it, the surer he was.

Spike gleeped again.

"What was that noise?"

"Cool it," Alastair said under his breath.

"Cool wha…." Josh said again. He never forgot anything.

Alastair sent him a look that meant cool it until later. This time Josh got it.

"Oh," he said. "Want a comic?"

Alastair shook his head. He couldn't read in a car. It was curious though that he could play computer games in a moving car, but they were not supposed to bring them along on this trip. Nowhere to plug them in when they set up camp or something like that. Sometimes mom wanted him to read books. He hadn't brought any. He'd forgotten them. Maybe comics would count as books, but he suspected they wouldn't.

He looked out the window. They were leaving Hilliard behind as they drove through the rolling green Virginia countryside dotted with horses and cows to Interstate 95 which would take them south to the Green Slime Swamp.

Chapter 3

Alastair leaned forward to talk to Uncle George. "How long before we get there?"

"Not until late afternoon."

"What's the campground like?"

"Don't know. Haven't stayed at this one yet."

Alastair asked several more questions which Uncle George answered in only one or two words. This wasn't like him. Alastair guessed he had to concentrate on driving the van with the canoe and tent on top.

The silence stretched out like the Interstate. They stopped for lunch on the other side of Petersburg. Uncle George parked where they could watch the van from a window.

"I've been hungry since we left Hilliard," Josh said.

"That's because you're always hungry," Alastair said.

Uncle George laughed. Alastair didn't. He had never known Josh not to be hungry.

"What time will we get there?" Josh asked.

"The campground is deep in the swamp," Uncle George said. "We have to drive on some two-lane roads. That will slow us down, but our ETA should be a little before dark."

"ETA means estimated time of arrival," Alastair said. He waited for Uncle George to continue but he seemed more interested in his burger. The boys ate theirs and fries and made a pit stop.

Alastair climbed into the back of the van to check on Spike while Uncle George examined the fastenings on the canoe. He slid the zipper down partway. Spike was sleeping. Alastair fished Claudia's strawberry out of his pocket and left it by Spike's nose where he would find it when he woke up. Spike liked little snacks after his naps.

"What are you doing back there," Josh asked.

"Nothing. Just getting my notebook," Alastair said. He pulled it out from under Spike and zipped the duffle closed before Spike could make any indignant dragon noises that would give away the secret.

Josh gave him a suspicious look.

"All aboard!" Uncle George started the engine. He seemed more his usual self but when Alastair asked him questions about the Lizard Man, he seemed to be thinking about something else. Alastair hoped he wouldn't be like this for the whole trip.

They read comic books. Alastair doodled pictures of what he thought the Lizard Man might look like.

By mid-afternoon, Uncle George turned east toward the coat of North Carolina, then south. "The swamp straddles the state line between the two Carolinas," he explained as the road narrowed to a tunnel of intertwined branches and arching trees. Swoops of wild grapevines cloaked whole trees. Mirror strips of water stood on both sides of the road with ponds and pools glimpsed through breaks in the trees beyond. Josh abandoned his comics to stare at the strange scenery.

"Look at that," he said as they rattled over a narrow bridge spanning black water reflecting snaky trees.

"It looks like another planet," Alastair said, "planet jungle."

"Those vines look like giant snakes," Josh said. "Anacondas and boas and pythons."

"Anacondas live in South America," Uncle George said. "Pythons and boas that escaped in Florida seem to be staying down there because of the colder temperatures up here."

Uncle George stopped at a little store with gas pumps in front and a sign, Johnsontown Grocery. "Got to pick up the campsite permit here," he said.

Alastair and Josh climbed out of the van. It felt good to stretch their legs as they followed Uncle George.

"But where's the town?" Josh asked in a loud whisper.

"Died out," a man's voice said from the back of the store. He closed the door to another room as he came in the front of the store and behind the counter. "I'm Bill Johnson," he said. "I'm the last of the Johnson family to live here. Unless my nephew decides he doesn't want to live in the city anymore. What can I do for you folks?"

"I'm George McKnight. I reserved a campsite in the Green Slime Swamp."

"That's right. Got your letter around here somewhere." He riffled through a stack of papers by the register.

"Ah here it is. Here's your permit, all signed, sealed and paid for." He handed it to Uncle George with a flourish.

Uncle George put it in his pocket and bought a carton of milk for the boys.

"There's two more camps in the swamp this week," Mr. Johnson said, "but you probably won't even see them. It's a big swamp. They're the Columbia Botanical Society from Washington, D.C. and a horticulture society from Virginia somewhere. Looks like you're all from about the same place."

"It's a big state. Any more sightings of the Lizard Man lately?" Uncle George asked.

"Nope. Been quiet for awhile, but it wouldn't surprise me if there aren't some." Mr. Johnson smiled. "No sir. Wouldn't surprise me a bit."

They drove down a dirt road that was hardly more than a track. Branches scraped the sides of the van. Alastair had never been so far from civilization before. Anything could happen back here in this swamp. Anything could be living in these trees, that water, clinging to those vines.

Uncle George stopped in a clearing under twisty limbs hung with long gray Spanish moss. Nobody moved for a minute.

"Welcome to the Green Slime Swamp, boys," Uncle George said. He waved his hand at the thick wall of greenery threaded with silent unmoving black and green water.

"It's a jungle," Josh said. "I need a pith helmet and snake boots and stuff."

"Not here yet. Good." Uncle George said as he got out of the van.

"Who? Who's not here yet?" Alastair asked as his stomach started feeling funny.

Chapter 4

"I didn't want to spoil the trip for you, sport but you'll find out soon anyway. Your teacher, Ms. Cassowary. She found out about the expedition and insisted on coming along."

"Oh no!" Josh said as he almost dropped his duffle.

The funny feeling in Alastair's stomach did a flip then a flop.

He looked at Josh. This was awful. This was almost the worst thing in the world, to have their strict fourth grade teacher along on the camping trip. Alastair could imagine it. They would have to wipe their feet before going into their tents. They would have to eat their hot dogs with a fork. And use napkins. They might have to use fingerbowls.

They would have to use manners and hygiene and say please and thank you all the time. They would have to do all the things she made them do all year at school. She had probably brought along math fact sheets. And workbooks.

And when it was over, she would make them write reports.

And grade them.

She would know if they made anything up.

"Oh no!" the boys groaned together.

"How? How did she find out?" Alastair asked.

Uncle George shrugged. "I know how you feel, but she knows about the dragon now. We have to humor her."

Alastair tried to imagine Ms. Cassowary in her shiny crayon-colored high-heeled shoes that matched her dresses and pants in this swamp. The heels would sink into the soft earth. They would have to dig her out. "Maybe she won't stay long," he said.

"Maybe," Uncle George said but he seemed distracted, as if his thoughts were somewhere else.

Alastair didn't know how he was going to manage to keep Spike hidden from Uncle George, Josh *and* Ms. Cassowary. She had eyes in the back of her head, the soles of her shoes, her elbows, knees and everywhere else and knew things before they happened.

Uncle George cleared his throat and looked like he wished he were in somewhere safe like Nepal. "There's more."

"More?"

"What more?" Josh said.

"It's worse than that."

"Worse?" Dread gathered in Alastair's stomach like one of his mom's gelatin salads. How could it be worse when it was already as bad as can be with Ms. Cassowary watching their every move with all of her eyes?

"She's bringing her nephew."

"Ugh!" Josh looked at Alastair. They both were imagining the horrible creature her nephew would be, a cross between a know-it-all and a tattletale. Uncle George didn't know anything about the nephew, not even his age or where he lived, just his name, Sydney.

"Let's set up camp," Uncle George said, reaching for Alastair's bag.

Alastair leaped ahead of him. "I'll get it."

"OK, I'll call your mom to let her know we're here." Uncle George dug out his cell phone and clicked the number on his speed dial.

As Alastair lifted the bag, a distinctive *growff* came from within. Uncle George didn't notice but Josh did. He recognized the source of the *growff*. His eyebrows disappeared into his hair and his ears turned red. "Wow! You're really gonna be in trouble now."

"Not if you help me." They unloaded the bags and Uncle George's equipment while he chatted on the phone. Alastair took a quick peek in the duffle. Spike uncurled himself and stretched.

"Not yet, fella," He said, rezipping the bag.

Spike's indignant *mewfpsses* and *growflls* were lost in the canopy of insect noises that hung over the Green Slime Swamp.

The boys helped Uncle George clear the ground and set up a tent big enough for the three of them. They unfolded the three camp cots and left their rolled-up sleeping bags on top of each one. Next, they unloaded the canoe from the top of the van and tethered it to a tree where it floated on the smooth black surface of the swamp water.

"Why is it called the Green Slime Swamp?" Josh asked. "It looked like the Black Swamp to me."

"Because of the duckweed," Uncle George said. "Lemnoideae is part of the arum family which are lilies. It floats on the surface or under slow or unmoving water. Look through there," he pointed. "You can see a lot of it. That's duckweed."

In the distance the duckweed was so thick that the top of the water looked like green foam. "Some people think it's slime but it's really not. That's where the name of the swamp comes from." He reached into the black water and lifted a

23

handful of duckweed which proved not to be slime at all but a lacy floating plant.

"Pick it up," Uncle George said.

Alastair and Josh each put out a hand but before they could break the surface of the water it came alive with minnows zipping away. Josh snatched his hand back. Alastair didn't. He didn't know what might be in that black water. He didn't want to put his hand in it either but if he wanted to be a scientist like Uncle George he had to learn to do things like that. He spread his fingers just under the surface. The water was cool and clear, not black or even green. He scooped up a handful of the duckweed.

When nothing happened to Alastair, Josh tried it. Just as his hand went under the duckweed, something big hit the water nearby.

"Yeow!" Josh jumped backward about four feet.

"It was just a turtle or maybe a bullfrog," Uncle George said. "But be careful. There are alligators around here and water moccasins. Keep your eyes and ears open and don't lean over the water like you're doing now."

Alastair and Josh jumped back.

"Alligators!" Josh looked like he might faint.

"And no swimming."

No chance of that. Alastair hadn't even brought a bathing suit.

Alligators. Ms. Cassowary. Her nephew. Snakes. The Lizard Man who might not like people. The Green Slime Swamp was turning out to be a dangerous place.

When Uncle George sent them to gather wood for a campfire, "Lots of it, guys," Alastair ducked into the tent to give Spike a carrot in case he was hungry while Josh stood lookout. Spike made more grumpy noises, but grabbed the carrot with his front paws. He held it like an ice cream cone as he munched. His little round dragon eyes held questions Alastair couldn't answer. Questions like why was he having to sleep in a zippered bag? He wanted to run around and explore and play the way he did at home.

"Later little fella," Alastair whispered, hoping Spike understood.

Sunrays filtered through the dense green canopy of trees, washing the swamp with yellow light and suddenly it was gone as if something were sucking it away and the swamp turned into deep green gloom. At the same time a great noise started up, jillions of insects, frogs and who knew what else tuned up their instruments and began their evening swamp song.

"This place is spooky," Josh said.

Alastair agreed. They hurried to collect armloads of wood while they could still see. They dug a firepit and started a fire under Uncle George's direction as he unfolded a table and chair. He set his computer up and soon had it running on batteries. Now, Alastair decided, while Uncle George was busy would be a good time to take Spike for a walk. As he started toward the tent, he heard a noise and turned around.

Two eyes blazed in the dark.

Chapter 5

The eyes came closer.

Something nudged Alastair.

He yelped.

It was only Josh. "What-what's that?"

The eyes stopped just a few feet from the boys. Flaps shot out of the monster's dark sides.

"Sorry we're late," a familiar voice said over the noise of the swamp. A pair of feet swung out onto the ground, feet wearing day glo hot pink sneakers below jeans. The monster eyes went out and the person stepped into view.

The monster turned into an SUV.

The person turned into a monster.

"Hi boys." It was Ms. Cassowary. In jeans and those sneaks and a hot pink tee shirt. And dangly lizard earrings. Alastair was surprised her sneaks weren't high heeled and open-toed.

Feet got out of the other side of the SUV. Another pair of sneaks, also day glo hot pink. Sydney?

The nephew came into the light of the campfire. He had dark red curly hair like his aunt. He had on a pink tee just like hers. He had on dangly lizard earrings. Sydney wasn't a nephew. Sydney was a niece. How had Uncle George got it wrong?

A girl! Alastair and Josh looked at each other thinking the same thing. Not only a girl, but a girl related to Ms. Cassowary. Worse! A girl that was a miniature of Ms. Cassowary. This was too much.

Way too much.

Beyond way too much.

"This is my niece Sydney J. Abbott. These are the boys I told you about, Alastair and Josh."

Sydney grinned and stuck her hand out at Alastair. He jumped back as if she was about to zap him.

"Um, Alastair, where are your manners? It's customary to shake someone's hand when offered," Uncle George said.

Alastair made a great show of wiping his hand on his shorts. He shook Sydney's hand and was surprised at her strong grip. She didn't let go when he did. Her eyes had a devilish challenge in them. Oh no. How were they going to have fun with her around?

Josh was next. He wiped his hand off first too, but he grinned back which Alastair hadn't done and said, "Hi, Sydney. Hi, Ms. Cassowary."

Alastair didn't think he had to be such a suck-up. He was sharing his special camping trip with Josh and now Ms. Cassowary and Sydney were about to ruin it.

"This looks like a good place. I think we'll put our tent up here," Ms. Cassowary said as she surveyed the campground. It was straight across from their tent facing it. Sydney lugged a duffle over while her aunt carried the tent. Uncle George jumped up to help, but Ms. Cassowary told him they didn't need help, thank you. He looked relieved but not happy at the same time which puzzled Alastair. What was wrong with his uncle? Didn't they all hate Ms. Cassowary and by extension Sydney?

"Have you already eaten?" Ms. Cassowary asked. She glanced around, but there was no evidence of food.

"Um, no, not yet," Uncle George said rummaging in the cooler. "We haven't been here long. Um, we seem to have forgotten to bring hot dogs. Guess it's empty buns for us for dinner, sports." He looked pitiful holding the empty cooler.

"Nevermind," Ms. Cassowary said. "We have plenty of vegetarian dogs."

"Vegetarian dogs!" Alastair and Josh said as one.

Uncle George looked even more pitiful but veggie dogs were better than plain buns.

"Veggie dogs," Josh said under his breath.

Sydney gave them a look like she knew what they were thinking. Just like Ms. Cassowary. Same snapping black eyes.

Ms. Cassowary opened a large container of potato salad.

"Homemade," she said.

One whiff and the boys were almost drooling.

"Maybe they'll share that to," Josh whispered but loud enough for Ms. Cassowary to hear.

Uncle George opened his Swiss Army Knife and cut green sticks from nearby bushes for them to roast the veggie dogs on.

"If you'll remove your computer, we'll share all of our food with you," Ms. Cassowary said, holding an armload of things that smelled good. She nodded at the table.

"Oh um, yes, certainly." Uncle George whisked his computer away while eyeing a chocolate angel food cake.

"Guess it's not all bad," Josh whispered as they roasted the veggie dogs over the fire and shared Ms. Cassowary's baked beans and salad. Uncle George had forgotten mustard but he had two squeeze bottles of ketchup. Ms. Cassowary had everything needed for hot dogs. Homemade slaw. Three kinds of mustard. Two kinds of relish. Jars of olives and other kinds of pickles. And chopped onions.

Alastair started to reply but before he could speak, he heard a dull thumping sound from somewhere inside the tent. Spike!

He was jumping around in the duffle. Alastair checked but everybody was busy with their food. They didn't recognize the *grish growfffs* and whomps with all the other noises from the woods surrounding the camp.

Everybody but Josh. He raised an eyebrow over his third veggie dog.

"He has to poop," Alastair whispered but he didn't need to. Josh knew Spike's habits almost as well as Alastair.

He nodded. "Wait til everybody's asleep." Josh whispered to Alastair.

Grummppppppffff. Growfffffp. Grumfffffgrowfffffpppp!

Maybe they would think it was a frog or a gator. Or a turtle. Did turtles make noises? Alastair didn't think so but in this swamp anything could happen.

Maybe nobody would notice.

"Did you hear that?" Sydney piped up.

"What?" Alastair made his eyes look as innocent as he could which meant that he probably looked guilty. Ms. Cassowary would think so.

"That splash?" Josh asked.

"No, it wasn't a splash. More like some kind of growling animal."

"I didn't hear anything. Did you hear anything Josh?"

"No not me. Just the usual jungle sounds. I was busy chewing."

Sydney gave Josh a pained look. "I *heard* you chewing. People in Georgia heard you chewing. Maybe Tennessee. Over there I heard a growly noise." She pointed behind the tent.

"Aw, it was probably just something in the swamp," Josh said with his mouth full. "Just a 'ol gator or a panther or something like that."

"It could be the Lizard Man." She took a tape recorder out of her backpack and set it on the table. It was voice activated but there was so much noise in the swamp and the camp, it ran nonstop.

Alastair helped himself to another piece of cake and hoped Spike would go back to sleep.

"This is really good cake," he told Ms. Cassowary.

"Thank Sydney, Alastair. She made it."

"I made it with honey and coconut sugar," Sydney said.

Alastair wanted to spit it out but he didn't. It tasted too good.

Josh wolfed down his second piece. He pointed with his chin. Alastair turned to look. Sydney was going to her tent. Good. Maybe she was going to bed now. Maybe Ms. Cassowary would too. Maybe then they could have some guy time with Uncle George who was always a lot more fun than he had been so far.

Ms. Cassowary stayed where she was, next to Uncle George sharing a piece of cake with him. Who ever *shared* a piece of chocolate cake?

Things were bad but not as bad as they could be. Sydney came back aiming a camcorder at everybody.

"Hey—what're you doing?" Alastair said wondering why she didn't use her phone.

"Yeah, turn that thing off," Josh said.

"This is Sydney J. Abbott. I'm the official cameraperson for this expedition. I'm videoing the members of the expedition to find the Lizard Man in the Green Slime Swamp on the border of North and South Carolina," she said in a voice like a TV narrator.

Oh no she wasn't. Alastair swallowed a gulp of air. "You can't be. I'm the official cameraman. Tell her, Uncle George."

Uncle George looked uncomfortable. Ms Cassowary smiled encouragingly. Alastair couldn't tell who she was encouraging, but he bet it wasn't he, Alastair McKnight.

"Um, well, I guess you are, sport. Where's your camcorder?"

Alastair gave Sydney a look and went to the tent to get his camcorder. An awful sinking sensation hit him in the middle of his stomach where the two pieces of chocolate cake sat along with the rest of the camp food.

He remembered taking things out of his bag when he put Spike in while he was packing. Had he put everything back?

He checked his bags. Not in the backpack. He unzipped the duffle. Spike tried to leap out for his walk.

"Not yet, fella," he told the dragon as he tried to put him back in. He felt all around in the bag.

Grumppp. Growffff.

No camcorder.

Sydney won. Nothing he could do about it. A cameraman without a camera wasn't like a pilot without a plane. A pilot was still a pilot. He had a piece of paper saying he was a pilot. Alastair had no such thing. Without a camera, he was only Alastair McKnight. Forgetful boy.

He went back to the fire.

"Well, sport," Uncle George said.

"Um, I must have forgotten it," he mumbled.

Sydney lifted her chin. Smug was written all over her face from her smirky smile to her superior eyes under her raised eyebrows. I-have-a-camcorder-and-you-don't. She clicked record and said in her narrator's voice, "The official cameraperson for the expedition is still Sydney J. Abbott."

Chapter 6

As the flames burned low in the campfire, Uncle George told them about the sightings of the Lizard Man. "He's been seen at least fourteen times over a period of three years."

"Wait!" Sydney pulled out a notebook and pen. "I want to get that down."

"You can't film and write at the same time," Alastair said.

"Yes I can. I want it recorded *and* on paper. I like to be thorough. I'll put the cam on record and I can write fast. I write in cursive." She set the machine on the table facing Uncle George, then sat in range of the lens. "OK, I'm ready."

"How does she do that?" Josh mumbled through his cake.

"What?"

"Talk in italics?"

Alastair rolled his eyes as if it were obvious. Sydney was a girl. She was Ms. Cassowary's niece. Those were only two of the most obvious explanations.

Ms. Cassowary also took out a notebook and pen. She held the notebook on her lap. "Today is June 23." She looked expectantly at Alastair and Josh as if they too should be taking notes.

Sydney wrote the date on the first page of her notebook.

Alastair could remember what Uncle George said. He and Josh remembered everything his uncle told them because it was so interesting.

"Have all the sightings been in the Green Slime Swamp?"

"Good question, Sydney," Uncle George said. "So far they have. The last five sightings were in the spring of this year and last."

Sydney's pen made scratchy sounds that made Alastair itch.

"When was the last one?" she asked without looking up from her notebook.

"April and May."

She was full of questions.

Alastair tried to think of some. Or one.

He searched his mind.

It was blank.

"Where were the sightings?" Ms. Cassowary asked.

"Here. Some birders were camped here in this campground. The Lizard Man stepped out of the woods. The birders ran away."

Everybody was quiet for a minute. The Lizard Man could be watching them.

Now.

This very minute.

Alastair stared at the darkness dotted with fireflies blinking around them. So did Josh. It looked like the woods were winking at them.

Josh raised his hand.

Alastair elbowed him. "You don't have to raise your hand. We're not in school."

Josh ignored him.

"Yes, Josh." Uncle George waited.

Josh put his hand down. "What are birders?"

Alastair knew that but Sydney got her hand up first.

"People who look for birds. They keep lists of their sightings and go on trips to places like the Green Slime Swamp to look for them."

"That's right," Uncle George said.

Ms. Cassowary looked proud of her niece. A chip off the family block.

Josh had another question. "How big is the swamp."

Alastair knew the answer to that too. "Huge. The Green Slime Swamp is huge."

"If you count all the tributaries of the Noire River, it's nearly three hundred square miles."

"That is huge," Ms. Cassowary said.

"Um, what's a tributary?" Josh asked.

Good 'ol Josh. That's what friends are for—to keep you from looking stupid in front of Ms. Cassowary and Sydney.

Alastair cut his eyes at Josh and flashed him an 'I owe you, dude' look. Josh ignored him. Maybe he didn't know it was a stupid question.

"I know! I know!" Sydney waved her hand in the air. The one with the pen. "It's the streams and creeks and smaller rivers that feed into the Noire."

"I knew that," Josh said.

"I certainly hope you did," Ms. Cassowary said, "or a lot of last year was wasted. We covered tributaries in the unit on the western expansion. Remember the discussion over whether the Mississippi River is a tributary of the Missouri River or the Missouri a tributary of the Mississippi?"

"Oh sure," Josh said. "I just didn't know there was a discussion about the More River."

"It's the Noire," Sydney said. "No-wire. That's French. It means black."

"Yes, it does," Uncle George said with a smile.

"Duh, anybody could tell that," Josh said. "That water is as black as night."

"What are some of the tributaries of the Mississippi River?" Ms. Cassowary asked.

Sydney flapped her hand again, this time without her pen.

"Ohio," Alastair said. He didn't know where it came from, but he remembered some kid named Huckleberry passing it on a raft going down the Mississippi.

"Excellent." Ms. Cassowary nodded encouragement. "What else?"

Alastair couldn't remember what else. He wished he were on a raft on the Mississippi. A raft with Spike on it. And Josh. And nobody else. Maybe Uncle George. The old Uncle George. Not this one.

Ms. Cassowary let Sydney answer. She rattled off the names of those rivers like she was counting out for hide and seek. "Arkansas, Des Moines, Kaskaskia, Rock, Wisconsin, Iowa, Galena and—" she glanced at Alastair and Josh as if they reminded her of something and said, "Oh yes, the Skunk."

"Correct, Sydney," Uncle George said, "and many creeks too numerous to name run into the Noire."

"Three hundred square miles is pretty big," Sydney said, consulting her notes by fire and lantern light.

Whoop-de-doo, Alastair thought. Anybody would know that.

Josh rolled his eyes. His eyeballs were getting a workout.

"I read up on lizards," Sydney said.

She would, thought Alastair.

"I have a few questions about them."

"OK," Uncle George said. "Fire away."

Sydney consulted her notes. Alastair tried to read them. The long page was covered with a lot of little bitty writing. Why did girls write so tiny? How could she read her own writing? This could take all night. His dragon couldn't wait that long.

"Do you think he's more man or lizard?"

Uncle George looked thoughtful. "That's one of the questions we're here to answer, assuming of course that the Lizard Man is real and not a hoax or a joke."

"A hoax?" Josh.

"It means fake," Alastair answered.

"Meaning to deceive," Sydney corrected with a toss of her head.

"That's right. Some people have nothing better to do than think up ways to fool people into believing things. Like the Piltdown Man," Uncle George said.

"What's that?" Josh asked.

"In 1912 some people found bone fragments in England that they said were those of prehistoric man. In 1936 with the invention of radiocarbon dating, the bones were found not to be prehistoric at all."

"So somebody could be dressing up in a lizard suit and running around in the swamp?" Ms. Cassowary said.

Alastair was horrified. The Lizard Man a fake?

"That's one possibility," Uncle George said.

"I don't believe he's a hoax," Alastair said.

"Me, neither," Josh said.

Sydney's grin looked like a jack o'lantern in the firelight.

"The Lizard Man has been sighted in many areas of the Green Slime Swamp," Uncle George said. "This would probably indicate that it's not a hoax unless more than one individual is doing it. In that case, the descriptions would probably vary. So far they have been uniform."

"That means the same," Sydney said.

"Duh," Alastair and Josh said but under their breaths.

"Do you have a map with the sightings marked?" Sydney asked.

"Yes, I plotted the sightings at the Institute. The most numerous sightings have been here around Johnson Creek. That's why we're camping in this area. Tomorrow we'll start looking for signs of him. They'll be plenty of time for questions as we search. For now, I suggest we turn in so we can get an early start."

Alastair jumped up. That was fine with him if it ended this show-off session with Ms. Know-it-all.

He was mad at himself for not thinking of any questions. He was the one who was going to be a scientist like his uncle. Maybe he should have thought up some before they came. He would have to try before tomorrow.

For now his mind was on taking care of Spike. That's why he couldn't think of any questions. He would take care of Spike tonight. Tomorrow he would be full of questions.

Just you wait, Sydney J. Abbott.

Chapter 7

Alastair slunk off to the tent. This trip wasn't turning out as he had expected. He unzipped the duffle to get his toothbrush.

Zheeepppp! Spike chirped as he leaped out ready to romp.

"Shhhhh, not yet fella." Alastair caught Spike in midair and pushed him back into the bag. He felt terrible as he zipped it up. The poor little dragon had been cooped up since this morning. He was probably hungry, thirsty and needed to potty in the worst way.

"Sydney is the pits," Josh said as he squeezed toothpaste on his toothbrush.

Alastair nodded, his mouth foamy. He rinsed with bottled water and took off his sneakers but didn't change into pajama bottoms and tee that he slept in on camping trips. Instead he got his flashlight out of the other bag. This day wasn't over yet.

The night was too warm to get inside his sleeping bag. He lay on top of it, trying to ignore the movements of his duffle bag. He would sneak Spike out for dragon latrine as soon as it was safe.

Josh eyed Alastair's clothes and only took off his sneakers too. Alastair didn't have to tell him why.

Meuwf. Meuwf. Meuwf.

Neglected baby dragon sounds that were swallowed up by the noise of the swamp unless you knew what to listen for.

Meuwfff. Meuwfff. Meuwffffffff!

Desperate baby blue dragon sounds.

"Shhh. I'll take you out in a few minutes."

Growfell! Growfell! Growfellllllll!

"Not yet, Spike."

Thwomppppp. Spike slammed something around in the bag. Alastair hoped it wasn't something breakable.

"Be quiet, please, Spike. Uncle George is coming. I'll take you out as soon as I can."

Uncle George seemed to take forever to get ready for bed. Finally he said, "Night, sports," and turned in.

The duffle made rustly mewy noises. Did Uncle George hear them? He didn't seem to. All around the tent frogs and insects thrummed and croaked and fiddled. In a few minutes

Uncle George added his snores to the swamp sounds. The other tent was quiet.

Now. Alastair nudged Josh. They pulled on sneakers. Alastair slid the zipper open on the bag. He lifted out the indignant dragon and slipped out of the tent. As he set Spike on the ground, Uncle George's cell phone rang.

Alastair leaped back in the tent and pounced on it before the phone could complete its first ring. He hurried back outside so he wouldn't wake Uncle George. Josh followed.

"Hello," Alastair whispered.

It was his mother. "Why are you whispering?"

"Everybody's asleep but me."

"I'm sorry I woke you up. I wouldn't have called so late if it wasn't important." She had discovered Spike was missing.

"No, he's not." Alastair explained why he had brought Spike along. "I couldn't have him not eating for weeks."

Good old mom. She understood. She promised not to mention Spike's whereabouts to Uncle George but laughed when she heard about Ms. Cassowary and Sydney.

"Let me get this straight. George has to put up with Ms. Cassowary and her niece on this expedition and you have to hide the dragon from everybody? Not from Josh. Well, that certainly makes things easier." She hung up still laughing.

Alastair didn't see what was so funny.

He put the cell phone back and joined Josh outside.
"Where's Spike?"

"I thought you had him."

"No, I put him down and then answered the phone."

Alastair pulled his flashlight out of his pocket and ran it through the darkness around the tent. No dragon.

"Spike?" he whispered in the dark.

No reply. No mewffs or growffs. No other dragon sounds.

"Do you hear him?"

"No, but the swamp is so loud he could be screeching his tonsils out and we wouldn't hear him."

"Thanks. That helps a lot."

"It's the truth."

Alastair didn't need reminding. Spike was missing in a gazillion miles of jungly swamp full of alligators, snakes, the Lizard Man and who knew what other kinds of monsters.

They crept around the camp area, searching as quietly as they could. They checked the perimeter of the other tent, under the van and the SUV, and on top of both.

No dragon.

"Over here," Josh said.

"Where? Did you find him?"

"No, but there's a sort of path. Maybe Spike found it."

Alastair aimed the flashlight beam along the path and the tangled swampy plants beside it. A lot of green but no blue.

Josh grabbed him. Alastair turned around to tell him to let go. He stopped with his mouth open.

Someone was coming.

Or something.

Someone was behind them on the path.

Someone with one eye.

One ghostly greenish eye.

The Lizard Man?

Chapter 8

Alastair turned his light on the eye and discovered that he was flashlight to flashlight with Sydney J. Abbott.

"What're you doing out here?" she demanded.

"What are you doing out here?" Alastair parroted.

"I heard a noise."

"So did we," Josh said.

Sydney flashed her light around on snaky things, trees, vines, leaves, bushes and roots.

"I don't see anything," she said.

"Yeah, let's go back to bed," Alastair said.

"It probably wasn't the Lizard Man," Josh said.

Alastair and Josh pretended they were going back to bed in their tent. They would sneak out later when Sydney was asleep.

They didn't have to. Spike was curled in Alastair's sleeping bag when he crawled in it.

Jzeep! Spike said, his curly little mouth smiling sleepily as Alastair snuggled in beside him.

Alastair fell instantly asleep with relief, Spike snuggled up against him just as he did at home. He was glad he'd brought his dragon along. It had been the right thing to do. They were both happier together.

At dawn, Alastair woke. Spike emitted steady dragonish snores that sounded a lot like purring. Before the others were up, Alastair took the sleepy Spike out to dragon latrine, then fed him a leftover veggie dog. Spike sampled a swamp flower but spat it out—ptui—and made a dragon face with the ends of his mouth turned down. He drank fresh water from Alastair's tooth cup. He didn't seem to mind the minty toothpaste taste.

Alastair stashed Spike in his duffle with a celery stick for a snack as the camp woke up for breakfast. He just had time to dive into his sleeping bag when Uncle George gave a great yawn and sat up. Ms. Cassowary came out of her tent, already dressed in crisp khaki shorts and shirt. She took a deep breath and said, "Ahh, fresh swamp air!"

Alastair shook Josh. "Come on, Josh, time to get up."

"Grumpff." Josh sounded like Spike as he turned over and burrowed back into his pillow.

"Yeeeeooooowwww!" A horrified scream came from the other tent. Uncle George, Alastair and Josh scrambled out of theirs and raced across the clearing.

Alastair expected to see Sydney being chewed up by an alligator.

Or squeezed by a boa constrictor.

But then, he reasoned, she couldn't have yelled that loud if all the air was being squeezed out of her. He settled for the alligator.

They crowded at the tent entrance and stared.

No alligators.

No snakes.

No blood.

Just Sydney balanced on one foot. The other sock-clad foot dangled in the air, goopy green stuff dripping from it in loud plops.

Alastair's eyes traveled from the end of her foot to the sneaker on the ground beside her cot. A sneaker filled with more goopy green stuff. Alastair knew what it was. He'd seen it before.

Dragon poop.

Somehow Spike had sneaked into the tent during the night and pooped into her sneaker. It wasn't the first time Spike

51

had used a shoe. He had ruined Alastair's brand new pair when he first came to live with the McKnights.

It might not be the last. Alastair bet Spike knew he didn't like Sydney. That was why he chose her sneaker out of all those in the camp.

He was glad Spike hadn't pooped in Ms. Cassowary's shoe but she might be next if he didn't take steps.

"What did this?" Sydney screeched.

"Some animal," Ms. Cassowary said.

"Oh, definitely," Uncle George agreed. He gave Alastair a thoughtful look. Did he suspect? Alastair tried to remember if Uncle George had ever actually seen dragon poop.

Meanwhile, Sydney's face had turned red.

"SOMEBODY DO SOMETHING!" she yelled in capital letters.

Josh pushed in behind Alastair and got a look at the green poop. "That's a..." Alastair stepped on his toe.

Didn't Josh ever think?

"Ow," Josh started to protest. Then he snickered.

Alastair couldn't help it. He laughed, too. Ms. Cassowary didn't but Alastair thought she wanted to. Uncle George managed not to laugh but he couldn't stop the corners of his mouth from turning up.

Sydney was outraged. "STOP LAUGHING AND DO SOMETHING. RIGHT NOW!"

Uncle George sent the boys for buckets of swamp water. They made sure to include some of the floating green stuff. Sydney didn't want to put her foot in it so they cheerfully took turns sloshing swamp water over her foot. She could wash the sock herself.

They weren't doing that.

After she had washed her foot about 2,000 times and poured a whole bottle of mouthwash over it, she insisted on moving the tent. "I'm not sleeping where that green stuff has been," she said.

Uncle George told the boys to bury the shoe which they did, poop and all, using a stick to move it from the tent to the freshly-dug hole.

"RIP, sneaker!" Josh said.

"It had a good life," Alastair said.

"Here lies Pink Sneaker, dead of green slime poop," Josh said just before collapsing with giggles.

Alastair laughed until tears came.

"No more pink sneaks," Josh said.

Prematurely, as it turned out.

Sydney emerged from the moved tent. Her feet were purple. Purple socks and purple sneaks. She had changed into a purple tee and purple shorts. She looked like a grape.

"You look like a grape," Josh said.

That made her mad again.

He hadn't said a grape with red hair.

"Breakfast time," Uncle George called. She had to let it go.

She had forgotten to video the green poop. Alastair was glad because no poop looks like baby blue dragon poop.

She hadn't forgotten her questions. She pulled out her notebook as they ate cereal and bananas.

"Do you think the Lizard Man is smooth-skinned like the anole, salamander and chameleon?" she asked, "or do you think he has scales like the Gila monster, Australian goanna and the iguana?"

"First I think we need to establish what a lizard is," Uncle George said. "One of the animals you named isn't a lizard. Who can tell me which one and why it's not a lizard?"

Sydney wanted to raise her hand. You could tell the way her shoulders twitched but she didn't know.

Alastair did. He raised his hand.

"OK sport, which one?"

"Salamander."

"Why isn't a salamander a lizard?" Uncle George asked without saying if Alastair was right.

"Because it lives in water," Alastair said.

"Why does it live in water?"

Alastair stared at Uncle George. He wanted to say because salamanders like it but he knew that wasn't the right answer.

"I know, I know!" Sydney waved her hand high.

"OK, Sydney?"

"A salamander is an amphibian like frogs."

She grinned at Alastair and Josh when Uncle George said she was right.

A lucky guess, Alastair thought.

Josh slurped his cereal.

"What about Galapagos iguanas. Why aren't they amphibians?" Alastair said. He had seen a program about them on TV.

"Because they don't live in water," Sydney said smugly.

"What are lizards then?" Ms. Cassowary asked.

Alastair looked at Josh. What was this, a pop quiz?

Josh shrugged and went on slurping. Slurping could take care of any number of problems.

Sydney frowned down her nose as if she were checking her computer monitor. Alastair thought about lizards. Some had scales. Some didn't. What else had scales? Snakes. Well some of them. And snakes were—Alastair raised his hand just as Sydney said, "Reptiles."

"I knew that," Alastair said.

"Me, too," Josh said.

Sydney tossed her ponytails. They were tied with purple, something shiny and purple. Alastair never wanted to see purple again.

Josh raised his hand.

"You have a question, Josh?" Ms. Cassowary said.

"My cousin had a lizard once. I think it was an anole. When it shed, it peeled its skin off in one piece and then ate it. Do you think the Lizard Man does that? Peels his skin off and eats it? Unless he has scales."

"Then does he eat his scales?" Alastair added for more gross-out.

Ms. Cassowary wasn't grossed out. "Interesting questions."

Did they get an A?

"Whoa," Uncle George said. "Let's back up. We don't know if the Lizard Man has scales or smooth skin. We don't know anything about the Lizard Man except that he's been seen in the Green Slime Swamp. He's been described as greenish. Some reports say he's scaly, some don't mention scales. He walks on two legs. Some have reported that he seems to be watching them, maybe even spying on them. Some report tails. Some don't mention tails. Our job is to keep our eyes and ears open. Try to get a look at this creature if it exists. We are here to collect data. To get him on film if possible. And to try to communicate with him."

"Talk to the Lizard Man?" Josh asked.

"If he can talk. Lizards tend to be silent creatures," Uncle George said.

"Like snakes," Alastair said.

Ms. Cassowary stood up. "Camp duty time."

Breakfast was over. They cleaned up the camp and piled into the canoe.

Sydney carried the camcorder in its waterproof bag.

Josh had a disposable camera in a Baggy.

Alastair had—nothing. Some scientist he was.

Uncle George explained the canoe rules. "No standing. No jumping. No paddle-play. Paddles go in the water and out. No slinging water or splashing. No sudden movements. Everybody has to obey the paddler in the stern of the canoe. That's the back for those who don't know. The front is the bow."

He sat in the stern with Alastair in the bow and Josh in the middle. The boys had never paddled a canoe before.

Ms. Cassowary sat between Josh and Uncle George.

Sydney sat between Josh and Alastair. He didn't like her there. He could feel those Sydney eyes on his back like something crawling on him. He dipped his paddle on the left side, Josh on the right and Uncle George on either side to make sure the canoe went forward.

It did and mostly it went straight.

"Why do they get to paddle?" Sydney complained. "I want a turn."

"You can't paddle and film," Alastair said over his shoulder.

"That's right," Josh said, letting a few drops of water fly off his paddle onto her grape tee shirt.

"Unless you want to let us do the filming," Alastair said.

That shut Sydney J. Abbott up. No way was she giving up being the official photographer of the expedition.

The canoe skimmed along the water's surface. It reflected trees and sky where it wasn't covered by duckweed. Sometimes the lacy green weed stuck like curly parsley to the paddles. Butterflies grazed on wildflowers that looked like butterflies themselves. Alastair waited for Ms. Cassowary to ask them to name the butterflies and the flowers.

She didn't.

Sydney showed off anyway. "Oh look at that huge Monarch."

Or "That's a big Swallowtail."

"You have sharp eyes, Sydney," Uncle George said.

Alastair and Josh kept paddling. They had sharp eyes too
but they didn't comment on every butterfly in the Green
Slime Swamp. They weren't here to look for butterflies.
They were here to look for the Lizard Man.

"We're not really looking for anything in particular,"
Uncle George said. "We're letting the Lizard Man know
we're here.

"There's a whole flock of turtles," Alastair said pointing
with his paddle

"Turtles aren't a flock," Sydney said.

"What are they then?" Alastair said.

"They're um, ah, a school?"

Sydney didn't know. Alastair was thrilled. "Maybe
they're a herd."

"A crowd?" Josh offered.

"A flotilla?" Uncle Josh got into the act.

Even Ms. Cassowary offered. "An armada?"

The truth was nobody knew what a bunch of turtles were.

The canoe glided deeper into the Green Slime Swamp.
They spied two men in a glade. The men didn't look up just
waved over their heads as the canoe passed them. Sydney

aimed the camcorder and filmed them until they were out of sight.

"They must be the botanists from Washington," Uncle George said. "Studying plants, cataloging them, Mr. Johnson said."

"Not very friendly," Ms. Cassowary observed.

At noon Uncle George steered them to an island for lunch. The sat on a fallen tree they had checked for snakes. Lunch was peanut butter and jelly sandwiches and bottled water. Ms. Cassowary contributed lemon cookies.

Alastair and Josh wanted to explore the island.

"OK, but stick to the water," Uncle Josh said. "We don't want you to get lost in this swamp."

"We might never find you," Ms. Cassowary added.

Sydney got up with them. "I'm coming too. I'll need to film the Lizard Man if we find him."

Alastair and Josh looked at each other, then started off along the bank.

"Watch out for alligators," Ms. Cassowary called after them. "They like to bask on banks."

"And snakes," Uncle George said. "Remember not to put hand or foot where you can't see."

"Hey, wait up," Sydney said.

Neither Alastair nor Josh slowed. Gangs of minnows fled from the water's edge as they walked along it. They surprised a slew of turtles, a squadron of frogs and at least one bullfrog that jumped into the water with a cannonball-sized splash.

They didn't see any alligators, snakes or the Lizard Man.

Sydney tried to aim the camcorder and walk at the same time. She tripped over roots and grass loops and once almost dropped the camcorder in the water.

"You better be more careful," Alastair said.

"Yeah, if you drop it in the water, I'll be the expedition's official photographer with my Instacamera!" Josh said.

Behind Sydney's back, they slapped five.

Every few steps, they stopped to check the swampy jungle.

"I feel like somebody is watching me," Sydney said.

"It's just your imag—" Alastair started to say when a loud crack sounded overhead and something fell out of the tree almost on top of them.

Something with arms and legs.

And a head.

The head shrieked all the way down and then it was quiet.

Chapter 9

All three of them shrieked.

Sydney dropped the camera on Alastair's foot.

"Ow!" he hopped around holding it.

"Is it broken?" Sydney stopped shrieking to ask.

"I don't think so," Alastair said, putting his foot down.

"I meant the camera."

Josh picked it up. "It looks OK."

She snatched it back and started filming the khaki-colored heap that had fallen out of the tree.

It didn't look like the Lizard Man.

It looked familiar.

Like somebody Alastair knew.

He gulped. This was worse than Ms. Cassowary. It was even worse than Sydney. The khaki heap looked like—Mr. Hobson.

The heap raised his head. It was! It was Mr. Hobson!

"Mr. Hobson! What are you doing here?" Alastair and Josh said together.

"Leonard, are you hurt?" A short bouncy woman in khaki shorts and a khaki shirt rushed out of the jungle and clutched Mr. Hobson's arm. She sounded like she hoped he had broken something, an arm or a leg. She whipped the green scarf off her brown ponytail ready to tie it around some part of Mr. Hobson. "Can you move everything?"

"I-I-I-," Mr. Hobson sputtered, staring at the boys. His neck which went all the way up to his mouth without stopping for a chin quivered as he tried to speak. His red potatoey nose twitched with the effort. His normally smiley-mouth mustache turned down over the thin line of his mouth.

"Is it a stroke, Leonard?" she asked.

Before Mr. Hobson could speak more people came out of the swamp jungle, two more women and two men, all wearing khaki shorts and shirts and knee socks. Most wore jungle pith helmets like the ones Alastair had seen in movies about jungles and Africa.

They crowded around Mr. Hobson, loosening his collar, asking him where it hurt.

"It might be a seizure," one of the men said. He picked up a stick and tried to hold down Mr. Hobson's tongue.

"Glopp dghat!" Mr. Hobson yelled as he tried to spit out the stick and shake off all the people who were examining his arms and legs.

"Dat batt!" He flailed his arms at the group. They stood back and Mr. Hobson sat up.

"Blott goo dhabing bere?" he yelled at Alastair and Josh.

"Ptooey."

The stick flew into the air.

Everybody watched as the stick made a sky loop accompanied by a spray of Mr. Hobson's spit. The stick landed on Alastair's foot. The same one the camcorder had landed on. He jumped back. He didn't want Mr. Hobson spit on his sneaker.

"What are you doing here?" Mr. Hobson said in his normal voice with his normal glare.

"Oh Leonard, you're not hurt?" the bouncy woman said. She sounded disappointed as she retied the scarf around her pony tail.

Mr. Hobson stood up. He clapped his pith helmet back on his yam-shaped head. It covered his bald spot. "What, WHAT are you boys doing here? Did you follow me from Hilliard? Do your mothers know where you are?"

"No, Mr. Hobson," Alastair said.

"Yes, Mr. Hobson," Josh said.

"Who are you?" Sydney asked aiming the camcorder.

Mr. Hobson looked like he wanted to climb up in the tree again to get away from them but he didn't. "Which is it? Did you follow me here?"

"No, Mr. Hobson," Alastair and Josh said together.

"Do your parents know where you are?"

"Yes, Mr. Hobson," the boys said together.

"Well then will you kindly tell me what you are doing in the middle of the Green Slime Swamp?" he asked.

Alastair figured he was being sarcastic. It wasn't like Mr. Hobson to use the word kindly when speaking to Alastair and Josh.

Sydney stepped forward. "We're on a scientific expedition for the Photon Institute," she said with importance.

"That's right." Alastair and Josh nodded, glad to let Sydney talk to Mr. Hobson.

"By yourselves?" murmured the woman with the green scarf.

"No, our leader is Dr. George McKnight. My aunt, Rita Cassowary is with us. We're looking for the Lizard Man. Have you seen him?"

"The Lizard Man?" If Sydney had said Godzilla, Mr. Hobson couldn't have looked more surprised. Then he started laughing. "The Lizard Man! That's really rich. George McKnight taken in by that old rural folktale."

Alastair didn't like Mr. Hobson in the normal course of things but he really didn't like Mr. Hobson laughing at Uncle George. "He's not taken in by anything. He's here to investigate reports of recent sightings."

"To find out if they're true or not," Sydney said.

Alastair almost liked her for sticking up for Uncle George.

"That's just somebody who dresses up to scare people away from the swamp," said the man who had put the stick in Mr. Hobson's mouth.

Alastair wished he would put another stick in his mouth as Mr. Hobson laughed again and said, "The Lizard Man is a hoax."

"If it is, then Dr. McKnight will prove that too," Sydney said.

"This swamp is filled with rare plants, orchids, sundews, Venus flytraps," the stick man said. "Somebody may be trying to protect them by scaring people away."

"Nobody believes in a real Lizard Man," Mr. Hobson said. "There's no such thing."

The group of grownups laughed heartily. Alastair and Josh and Sydney didn't. Soon the grownups stopped. Silence fell as the two expeditions stared at each other. The members of the smaller one were mad but had been taught not to talk back to grownups so they settled for some light-duty glaring.

Not for long. Something crashed around in the bushes. The grownups moved closer together.

"It's the Lizard Man!" Alastair yelled.

"Run for your lives!" Josh yelled.

"He'll get us!" Sydney yelled.

As the Hobson group turned to run, Uncle George and Ms. Cassowary emerged from the bushes.

"Leonard, what a surprise," Uncle George said.

Mr. Hobson stopped in mid-run. He tried not to look embarrassed as he recognized them. The green scarf woman also stopped but the others ran right into their backs which almost sent them into a sprawling heap of khaki. All of the pith helmets fell off.

"You must be the members of the Horticultural Society we heard were working in the Swamp," Uncle George said.

Mr. Hobson threaded his way through the group and introduced the members of the Society, Tillie Troutman with the green scarf, Dr. Edgar and Mrs. Dorothy Smith, Arthur Goldglass and Marlene Watts.

"I hope you don't have that Teagle with you," Mr. Hobson said to Alastair, looking around in the bushes. "That animal is a menace to horticulture. Can't have him wrecking the rare specimens of plants here in the swamp."

Alastair wanted to tell him he didn't have anything to worry about. Spike didn't like swamp plants but then everybody would want to know how he knew that.

"What's a Teagle?" Sydney asked.

Alastair looked at Uncle George and waited for him to answer. "It's a breed of dog," he said after a pause.

"I've never heard of a Teagle." Sydney turned to Ms. Cassowary. "Have you?"

"Yes, I have," she said. "I definitely have heard of a Teagle." She was trying not to laugh as she turned away to flick a bug off her shorts.

At least she had kept her part of the bargain and not even told her own niece about Spike. Alastair felt a little better about having her along on the trip.

But not much.

Chapter 10

"Someone has been here," Sydney said when they returned to camp.

"How do you know that?" Ms. Cassowary said.

"I left my book on my cot and look where it is now." She pointed at the picnic table. The book was face down on it.

"Everybody check to see if anything is missing," Uncle George directed.

Alastair didn't dare unzip his duffle with Uncle George in the tent. Spike might leap out. Or make a dragonish noise that Uncle George would recognize.

"Nothing missing I can find," Alastair reported. He picked up the book on the picnic table. "What page were you on, Sydney?"

"84."

"Somebody was here all right," Alastair said.

"How do you know that?" Sydney said.

"Somebody stopped reading on page 251. We must have interrupted whoever it was. Nobody would stop reading Harry Potter on page 251."

They didn't find anything missing but things had been moved around just slightly. Alastair studied the ground around the camp. In several places he found some kind of print that hadn't been made by any of their sneakers.

"I'll set up the camcorder," Sydney said.

"Somebody might steal it," Josh said.

"I'll disguise it so nobody will know what it is."

"I thought we had some leftover dogs from last night," Ms. Cassowary said, rummaging in the food supply cooler.

"Er, I ate them," Alastair said and Josh said together.

"Which is it?"

"We each ate one," Alastair said, "but one was left."

Spike had eaten a veggie dog for breakfast. But only one. One had been in the cooler when they left in the canoe. If he didn't eat it and Josh didn't, who did? The intruder?

"Could the Horticultural Society have been here?" Sydney asked.

"Or the Botanical Society?" Josh said.

"Not likely," Uncle George said. "They were all deep into the swamp by the time we found them. They wouldn't have had time to come here and get in front of us again. It was probably somebody passing by looking for money maybe or just checking us out. Or an animal nosing around."

"Anyway, no animal could have opened that cooler," Alastair said.

"A raccoon could," Sydney said.

"Not likely," Uncle George said. "They would leave more evidence."

"Raccoons don't read," Alastair said.

"So it had to be human," Sydney said.

Alastair ignored her. He wanted to get back to Spike but Uncle George sent him and Josh to collect more firewood. Sydney went with them. As they picked up sticks, Alastair's eye was caught by a color on a tree root. It was a scale, greenish-blue in color. It must be one of Spike's. He slipped it into the pocket of his shorts.

When he looked up, Sydney was watching him suspiciously. "What did you find?"

"Nothing."

Sydney stuck to Alastair and Josh like a leech especially Alastair, asking tons of questions.

"Who's Mr. Hobson? What kind of horticulturist is he? Do you think he's really looking for rare plants and orchids? Maybe they're planning to steal them. You know, orchidnappers."

71

Alastair and Josh looked at each other and groaned. "Who would nap orchids?"

"I've read about them," Sydney said. "People can become millionaires for finding new types of orchids."

Mr. Hobson would like that, Alastair thought, but he wouldn't steal orchids. Mr. Hobson didn't have any orchids. It was probably the only plant he didn't have.

He wished everybody would hurry up and get whatever they were doing done. He needed to take Spike out to feed and water him and let him do his dragon latrine.

Finally after a spaghetti supper, more questions from Sydney about the Lizard Man and more computer time for Ms. Cassowary and Uncle George, some reading time for Sydney, Alastair and Josh, everyone went to bed.

Alastair waited for Uncle George to fall asleep. His uncle was restless. He tossed and turned and mumbled in his sleep. "Not this time, Ri…"

"Ri…?" Alastair waited a little longer to make sure he was asleep.

The swamp surrounded the camp with its music as Alastair slipped out of the tent to the food stash in the van. He eased open the back door, felt around in the dark for the dragon food. Then he went back for Spike. He slid the zipper back on the duffle bag.

"Sorry little guy," he whispered waiting for Spike's fuming and fussing to start.

Nothing.

Frantic now, Alastair searched the duffle.

No dragon.

"Spike?" he whispered.

No answer.

Spike was gone.

He felt sick. Josh got up and joined him outside the tent. When they were out of sight of the camp, Josh said, "Where is he?"

"If I knew he would be with me. He was there this morning. The duffle was zipped when we got back. I thought he was safe and all this time he'd been outside, maybe stolen."

"Do you think the intruder got him?"

"Don't even say that!" Alastair didn't know what to do. He put the food down on the ground, a carrot and a handful of dry cereal and sunflower seeds. They were far enough from camp that it wouldn't attract bears or other wild animals to their food supplies if Spike didn't find it. If he didn't, Alastair didn't know what he would eat.

"We've got to find him," he said.

When they had gone far enough that nobody in the camp would hear them they called Spike and flashed their lights around.

Suddenly a light flashed over them as Sydney jumped from a bush behind them. "Aha! Caught you," she said just before letting out a screech that people could hear back in Hilliard, Virginia. "The Lizard Man! It's the Lizard Man!"

"Where? Where?" Josh and Alastair flashed their lights around but only saw swamp.

Uncle George raced along the path, followed by Ms. Cassowary in a shiny yellow bathrobe. Like satin. A shiny yellow bathrobe? On a camping trip? If you had to bring a bathrobe it should at least be like a towel. Her red hair crackled over the silk, bright as sunrise.

"Can you describe him?" Uncle George said.

"He's horrible! He has red eyes, blue scales. Claws." Sydney shuddered.

"Not green scales?"

"They could have been bluish green," Sydney said.

Alastair and Josh didn't even bother to look at each other. They knew what she had seen.

Alastair felt enormous relief. His dragon was nearby and safe. Maybe he was eating his food now.

Sydney had seen him. That could be a problem but so far she thought he was the Lizard Man.

"Did you boys see him?" Uncle George asked.

Josh shook his head.

"No, we were around that tree. Sydney was on this side. By the time we looked, he was gone. We flashed our lights around but didn't see anything. He must have run away," Alastair said.

"What were you three doing in the woods anyway?" Ms. Cassowary said.

"I was following them," Sydney said.

"Er, we were, you know, answering nature's call," Alastair said.

"Yeah, we had to—" Josh added.

"We understand," Ms. Cassowary said, cutting him off.

Uncle George divided them into groups of two and had them search with flashlights, but all they found was a raccoon in a tree. Its eyes glowed red in the lights.

"Sorry, Mr. Raccoon," Ms. Cassowary said.

"I bet that's the one that got the veggie dog," Sydney said.

He would get Spike's food too, Alastair thought if Spike didn't get it first.

"Let's go back to camp," Uncle George said.

"Did you hear that?" Josh turned around.

Something thrashed around in the jungle. They all stood still, listening. The sound moved away becoming fainter until it disappeared.

"Could have been a deer," Uncle George said.

"Or the Lizard Man." Sydney grabbed the camcorder and aimed at the bushes.

"Or a dragon," Josh said under his breath.

Alastair elbowed him.

"A what?" Sydney said, giving them a sharp look.

"Imagination," Alastair said.

Sydney sent him a fierce scowl. "It was not my imagination. I'm a scientist. I don't have any imagination."

Uncle George grinned.

Ms. Cassowary coughed. "Bedtime, everybody."

Alastair and Josh hung back.

"What are we going to do?" Josh said.

"I don't know. Maybe he'll come back like he did last night. If he doesn't, I'll have to think of something," Alastair said. He didn't know what that would be. If he didn't think of something he might never see his dragon friend again.

If Uncle George found out he'd lost the dragon, he'd never let Alastair go on expeditions again. And if they ever found Spike, he would have to go live at the Photon Institute. Uncle George would insist on it.

Alastair hardly slept worrying about Spike lost in the jungle of the Green Slime Swamp.

Where the Lizard Man lived.

Chapter 11

Ms. Cassowary and Uncle George were cooking breakfast when Alastair got up. His stomach churned at the sight of food. He managed to choke down one of Ms. Cassowary's camp biscuits loaded with marmalade. He washed that down with orange juice from Ms. Cassowary's cooler.

Sydney was smug about being the only one to see the Lizard Man. Alastair and Josh knew she hadn't, but they couldn't say anything as Sydney recorded the sighting in her notebook. "Why don't you record it in yours?"

"We will," Josh said.

"Later." Alastair wasn't putting anything he knew was fake in his notebook.

"The events yesterday suggest the Lizard Man may be curious about how people live," Uncle George said as they cleaned up camp. "I'll leave a note on the table in case he comes back to the camp while we're away."

"What if he can't read?" Josh asked.

Alastair wished he'd thought of that.

"The note is in case he can read," Sydney said before Uncle George could reply. "Right, Dr. McKnight?"

Dr. McKnight?

"Quite right. Please call me George. Dr. McKnight sounds so formal."

"Aunt Rita doesn't allow me to call grownups by their first names. How about Dr. George?"

"How about Uncle George. I can be your honorary uncle."

Alastair was disgusted. Next Uncle George would be inviting her to visit him at the Photon Institute and go on future expeditions. Expeditions Alastair wouldn't be going on when Uncle George found out Spike was lost.

"Super, Uncle George." Sydney smiled at her new honorary relative.

Sickening.

"Josh calls me Uncle George as well."

"I do?" Josh looked surprised. Alastair stepped on Josh's toes to make him keep quiet. Josh never called Uncle George anything.

Alastair wanted to change the subject.

"That makes us cousins," Sydney told them later when Uncle George was on his computer and Ms. Cassowary was on hers.

"No, it doesn't," Alastair and Josh said.

"Honorary cousins," Sydney said.

"Not even honorary," Alastair said.

"Nope," Josh said. "Not even close."

"We'll see about that," she said with a note in her tone that made Alastair feel uneasy, like an earthquake was about to open up and he would fall in a crack and then it would close up with him still in there.

Alastair and Josh watched as Sydney set the camcorder up in her tent and aimed it out at the camp to film whoever might have taken the veggie dogs if they came back. She made a hole in a box they'd brought food supplies in and put that over the camcorder so that only the lens showed and not much of it. She piled another box and clothes on top of the camcorder box.

"There. Now it's disguised."

Alastair thought a thief would just throw everything off and look in the boxes. If it was a thief. It might be somebody who had lost his library card and wanted to read books. Or someone who hadn't paid his library fines and couldn't go back for more books.

Or it might be the Lizard Man who liked veggie dogs.

And Teagles.

Suddenly Alastair had a scary thought. Had the Lizard Man taken Spike? And if he did, where was it while they searched last night? Could Lizard Man climb a tree like Mr. Hobson?

What if Spike came back while they were gone? Now he had another worry. Spike didn't know he was supposed to stay hidden. He had probably only run away last night because of Sydney's screeching.

Alastair wanted to stay close to the camp to search for Spike but it would look suspicious if he didn't go in the canoe after waiting so long to come on this trip. He'd worked hard at school to make the grades for the trip. With Ms. Cassowary as his teacher, he'd had to work extra hard. Super hard. Harder than he would have had to work for any teacher in all of Hilliard, Virginia. Now he would never get to go on another expedition and his wonderful pet dragon friend was lost. Alastair felt more morose than before.

"Cheer up, sport," Uncle George said when he could speak to Alastair in private while the others were loading up the canoe. "You're not really related to her."

He thought that was what was bothering Alastair. He managed half a grin. It was the best he could do for now. Sydney was the least of his worries.

The paddled the canoe south this time but it could have been the same route they'd taken the day before. Everything looked the same to Alastair. Black and green water, green jungle, screeching birds and frogs and who-knew-what else. Except for the alligator they saw sunning itself on a bank in the distance.

"At least a six-footer," Uncle George estimated.

Sydney filmed it while Josh snapped a picture.

Everybody looked for the Lizard Man. Everybody but Alastair. He was looking for his lost dragon. Josh was looking for both.

Who cared about a Lizard Man when the best pet you ever had, the only pet—unless you counted fish and Alastair didn't because you couldn't pet a fish—that you ever had was lost?

Uncle George was cheerful, probably because he thought they'd had a sighting of the Lizard Man. "Nothing finer than paddling a canoe through a swamp on a spring day in Carolina," he warbled to some tune as he stroked them through the black water.

"You'll scare away the Lizard Man," Ms. Cassowary said.

"No, I think he needs to hear us, to know where we are so he will show himself."

"If you keep singing like that, you'll certainly flush him out. He'll want to scare you off to get rid of that awful racket." Ms. Cassowary smiled.

Uncle George didn't seem insulted. "Can't keep a guy from his singing," he sang.

The Botanical Society was at work on another island. They barely glanced up as the canoe glided by. "Any luck?" Uncle George called.

"Excellent," the taller one replied through his black beard.

It wasn't really an answer. Maybe they were too busy to talk.

Around the next bend, Ms. Cassowary said, "Weren't they clean-shaven yesterday?"

"Beards grow fast in the swamp," Uncle George said nodding at the long beards of curly gray Spanish moss, some so long they swept the water.

"Not that fast," Ms. Cassowary said. "They both have full black beards and moustaches today. We didn't see them from the front but I'm sure they were clean-shaven yesterday."

"It's another of the swamp's mysteries," Uncle George said.

They stopped for lunch on another island. Uncle George and Ms. Cassowary took a walk before eating their lunch.

Alastair bit into his egg salad sandwich. "Do you think he got this far?" he asked Josh.

"Who? Who got this far?" Sydney sneaked up on them.

"Why are you always sneaking up on us?" Josh asked.

"Why are you always sneaking off?" she countered.

The boys had no answer for that, not one that would be acceptable to Ms. Cassowary or her niece and probably Uncle George.

There was also no side-tracking Sydney J. Abbott.

"Who got this far? Far where?"

"Mr. Hobson. My neighbor we met yesterday."

"Oh him." She seemed only half-convinced.

Alastair went to work on Sydney. "He's always spying on us like you are. You're just like him."

"I am not. Anyway why does he spy on you?"

"We don't know," Josh said.

"He doesn't like kids, I guess," Alastair added.

"Why not?"

Alastair gave her the short version. "He thinks we'll wreck his old flowers."

"What was he doing up in that tree? I bet he's spying on something," Sydney said.

"Could be." Alastair tried to think what Mr. Hobson would be spying on. The only thing that came to mind was himself and Josh. And Spike, the Teagle.

"What does he do anyway?"

"He grows flowers. Prize flowers that he wins prizes for in flower shows." Sometimes. Sometimes he wins prizes when Gruesome and Spike don't run through his garden and trample or eat the flowers. And Mr. Hobson doesn't beat them to death with a rake trying to get at what he thinks are a pair of bad dogs.

"I still say he's an orchidnapper," Sydney said. "Let's ask Uncle George."

"I don't think Leonard would steal an orchid," Uncle George said when he and Ms. Cassowary came back.

Sydney looked unconvinced. "He had a sneaky little moustache," she said.

On the way back to camp late that afternoon, they met the horticulturists again.

"Sydney wondered what you are doing here," Alastair said to Mr. Hobson.

"Yes, she thinks you're an orchidnapper," Josh said.

Sydney turned bright red and glowered at Josh and Alastair.

Mr. Hobson looked like he was trying to decide between mad, insulted or amused. Finally he decided on amused. "Oh haha, no never orchidnappers. That's funny. Haha. I'm quite the opposite. We're here trying to protect the delicate plants from thieves."

Ms. Cassowary looked embarrassed. Maybe that was why she did what she did. She invited the whole group over to supper. Alastair stopped himself from groaning aloud. Not supper with Mr. Hobson! It was bad enough to live next door to him. Alastair didn't want to have to sit across a fire from Mr. Hobson on a camping trip that was supposed to be fun and informative. Or eat supper with him.

"Yes, Leonard, Rita is an excellent cook, camp cook," Uncle George said. "You're in for a treat."

"Oh gag," Alastair said under his breath.

"What did you say, Alastair?" Ms. Cassowary fixed him with her piercing black eyes.

"Oh, gosh." Alastair scratched his leg. "Something just bit me."

She whipped out a tube of smelly green cream and insisted he put some on the bite. "Could be a mosquito bite. You can't be too careful in the swamp," she said. "The Englishman who discovered King Tut's tomb in Egypt, the Earl of Carnarvon had a mosquito bite on his cheek. He shaved with a rusty razor that nicked the bite. He died of blood poisoning and probably pneumonia three weeks later. There was nothing that could be done for infections in those days. Penicillin hadn't been discovered yet."

"Penicillin was discovered in 1928 by Alexander Fleming who grew a blue-green mold. By accident he discovered it stopped growth of bacteria," Sydney said.

"Who called on her?" Alastair muttered to Josh.

The talk turned back to swamp plants.

"People do try to nap rare orchids," Ms. Troutman said. "It's true. And also sundews and Venus fly traps."

"Why would anybody want to nap fly traps?" Josh asked.

"Not ordinary fly traps. A plant, Venus fly trap. Dionaea muscipula from the sundew family, Droseracaea. It's a plant that attracts insects to land on their sticky attractive leaves and then the leaves snap closed and the plant eats the flies," Mr. Hobson explained.

"Eeuw, a flesh-eating plant!" Josh said.

"Well, insect flesh," Alastair said.

He knew Spike wouldn't touch such a plant. Not his vegetarian dragon.

"We haven't seen many Venus fly traps," Dr. Smith said.

"Nor many orchids, either," Mr. Hobson said, "nor sundews. This has been a disappointing trip so far."

"The numbers have been way down," Dr. Smith said. "Far below expectations."

"What's the difference in horticulturists taking plants and plantnappers?" Josh asked.

"Oh dear me, we're not taking the plants," Ms. Watts said.

"No, we're merely doing a count of rare plants in our section of the swamp," Ms. Goldglass explained. "We're like bird watchers who make counts of birds, the number and types. We're counting rare plants in a grid that has been assigned to us in the swamp. So far we've found very few." He shook his head. "Very few."

"We hope people haven't been napping the plants. Or destroying them in any way," Mr. Hobson looked at Alastair in a meaningful way.

Alastair had never destroyed a single one of Mr. Hobson's plants. Or anybody's plants. Mr. Hobson always blamed him for the damage from Gruesome and Mr. Hobson himself as he chased the dog out of his garden. Alastair didn't think Spike would bother the rare plants. He hadn't seemed to like swamp plants. He preferred tasty dahlias and roses grown by Mr. Hobson.

All the way back to camp Alastair worried about his dragon. His own stomach growled as they paddled the canoe. He bet Spike was hungry. He hoped the dragon could find something to eat while he was lost in the swamp. Something besides orchids and sundews.

A growing dragon needed his food.

Chapter 12

When the canoe docked, Alastair rushed ahead of everybody to check the camp for Spike.

"Spike, Spike, where are you?" he whispered as loud as he dared, his eyes darting around the clearing and the tents.

No dragon.

Not even a sign of a dragon.

He checked for footprints.

No dragon prints. Just sneaker prints and those funny prints again.

Alastair slumped by the tent. He had been so sure Spike would be sitting in camp waiting for him. Why had Spike run away? Was he mad at Alastair? Maybe Spike didn't love him anymore. Or was he with somebody else? The Lizard Man maybe.

It was all a horrible nightmare. He wished he could wake up and find Spike snuggled in with him. Alastair only wanted the best for his super pet. Nobody else in the world had a pet like Spike. He had been trying so hard to take care of him, to do the right thing for his dragon and now Spike was lost. The Green Slime Swamp was a zillion miles square. He might never see Spike again. His dragon was lost where alligators and snakes and the Lizard Man and who knew what else was running around. His poor little dragon was all alone. He felt like crying as the others reached the camp.

A tear squeezed out from under his eyelids. He turned away but not in time.

"What's the matter with you?" Sydney asked.

"I got some of that stuff your aunt made me put on my mosquito bite in my eye. It's making it water."

Sydney didn't look convinced. "Never does that to my eyes."

"Maybe you didn't have it on your finger when you rubbed your eye."

Sydney went straight to the camcorder to check it.

The camcorder!

Alastair had forgotten about it. It had just filmed him calling spike. Alastair broke into a sweat. What would happen when Sydney looked at the film and saw him? She would really be suspicious. And Uncle George and Ms. Cassowary would know what he was doing.

The dragon would be out of the bag.

Maybe Sydney couldn't look at the film until she got home.

He and Josh collected wood again. It got them away from Sydney and gave them a chance to scout around for Spike.

"What'll you do if you don't find him?" Josh asked as they searched under vines and behind trees.

"We'll find him," Alastair said. "We have to."

"If you don't, you'll have to tell Uncle George or go back to Hilliard without him."

Go back without Spike? Alastair couldn't do that. He would run away into the swamp and keep looking forever if he had to.

Something crashed in the bushes reminding them they had been sent to collect wood. Alastair grabbed a stick. Josh did the same. They picked up an armload each and were on their way back to camp when they met Sydney.

"Uncle George said to hurry up," she said.

"We're coming," Josh said.

"We have to go farther each time," Alastair said. "It's not like a fresh crop of firewood sticks fall after we pick them up."

"I know that," Sydney said.

Ms. Cassowary and Uncle George made a feast out of canned ham with sweet and sour sauce, baked beans, vegetable salad and camp biscuits with more jam. It was almost ready when the Horticultural Society joined them bringing cheese spreads and crackers.

Mr. Hobson sat as far from the boys as possible and remain in South Carolina. From time to time he cast suspicious looks at them as he chewed. Sydney sat next to him and asked him questions about horticulture.

At first he looked pleased. The thin lines of his mouth turned up under his moustache.

After awhile Alastair noticed that Mr. Hobson was edging closer to him and Josh who would never ask him a single question or even speak to him if they didn't have to.

Could it be that Mr. Hobson would rather sit by them than by Sydney?

Strange things were happening in this swamp.

"Do you really believe in this Lizard Man you're looking for?" Mr. Hobson asked Uncle George.

"I don't believe or disbelieve. I'm here to search for data. Not all that different from what you're doing with the orchid and rare plan count. The Lizard Man has been sighted many times in the area. An old legend in these parts about prehistoric creatures living in the Green Slime Swamp, half man, half lizard. It's described as having a pointed head,

hooded eyes, green skin of scales—the accounts vary here—
and probably a tail," Uncle George said.

"Well, if anybody believes that stuff." Mr. Hobson
snorted. "I've got a nice second-hand bridge I'd like to sell
you. It goes from Brooklyn to Manhattan."

"We never knew you owned a bridge," Josh said. "We
thought you worked for the railroad."

"Do you charge people to go across it?" Alastair asked.
He knew by the way Ms. Cassowary laughed that he didn't.

Uncle George ignored Mr. Hobson's feeble attempt at a
joke. "My job is to check out these rumors and legends. This
one has been around for awhile. If such creatures exist, they
appear to be guardians of the swamp, chasing off explorers,
settlers, loggers, anybody that might disturb the pristine
natural area."

"Um, what does pristine mean?" Josh whispered to
Alastair.

Before he could reply that he didn't know, Sydney piped
up. "It means unspoiled. Right, Aunt Rita?"

Ms. Cassowary nodded. What did Sydney do, read the
dictionary at night?

Ms. Cassowary probably gave him and Josh bad grades
for not knowing.

They would flunk expedition. Alastair would flunk it anyway if they found out he'd brought Spike along. And for sure when they found out he'd lost Spike.

"Surely somebody would have taken pictures of such creatures if they exist," Mrs. Smith said.

"Even the Loch Ness monster has been photographed," Ms. Troutman said.

"It's not that easy to get a picture of an elusive creature that may not think like a human," Uncle George said. "That's what we're here for."

"And I'm the official photographer," Sydney said. "I'm the one who will film the Lizard Man when we find him. Isn't that right, Uncle George?"

Did she have to say Uncle George all the time?

"The problem with ordinary people photographing such creatures is that they are so shocked when they see one, they drop their cameras or run away or stand frozen until it's too late," Uncle George continued.

"I won't do that," Sydney said.

"I bet," Alastair said.

Josh snickered.

Sydney glowered at them.

ROWARRRRRRRRRRRRR came out of the dark. It was a horrible sound. It seemed to surround them. Suddenly a pair of eyes like ruby lights glowed against the green vegetation as something moved closer to the campfire.

A body appeared.

It gleamed with green scales.

Its claw-like hands snatched at the air.

Chapter 13

For an instant nobody moved. They couldn't. Alastair felt like he had turned to stone and grown roots at the same time.

The horticulturists moved first. They jumped up and ran in the other direction.

Uncle George seemed to be watching with a quizzical look as if he didn't believe what he was seeing.

Ms. Cassowary grabbed Sydney who was trying to pull her in the direction the others had taken.

The creature roared again and backed into the jungle, leaving behind a last ROARRRRRRR that seemed to bounce off the tents and Alastair's ears.

Ms. Cassowary threw an armload of wood on the fire. It blazed up lighting the clearing, reaching into the swamp's darkness with its warm friendly light.

The creature was gone. Still clutching each other, the horticulturists came back to the fire.

"What was that?" Mr. Hobson's eyebrows had almost disappeared under his pith helmet.

"It was the Lizard Man," Ms. Troutman said.

"And I've got its picture!" Sydney said.

"How?" Josh asked.

Alastair wondered too but hadn't wanted to ask. "You don't even have a camera," he said.

"The Camcorder is still recording." Sydney went in the tent and brought it back to the clearing.

"You've had it on all day," Alastair pointed out. "It's surely run out of film or juice by now."

"It's motion activated," Sydney said with a smug grin. She patted the camcorder. "It only films when something is close enough like we were." She opened the camcorder to check and her mouth fell open.

The camcorder was empty.

"Who took the film out?" Sydney whirled around to accuse Alastair and Josh.

"I didn't," Alastair said.

"I didn't either," Josh said.

"Then who did?"

"A good question," Ms. Cassowary said.

Alastair had a hard time not laughing at Sydney's face because she always asked such good questions but this time she hadn't meant to. He was relieved that she didn't have film of him coming into the camp looking for Spike. What luck was that? Maybe he would find Spike soon.

"We had another visitor while we were away," Uncle George said.

"The camp seemed unchanged," Ms. Cassowary said.

"Yes it did," Uncle George agreed.

Alastair remembered the prints he'd seen in the dirt. He hadn't seen any dragon prints, just sneakers and those funny ones that didn't look like any he had ever seen. Lizard Man prints?

He glanced at the horticulturists. Dr. and Mrs. Smith wore sandals and socks. The others including Mr. Hobson wore sneakers or running shoes.

"We had a visitor yesterday," Ms. Cassowary explained to them, "but nothing was taken."

Nothing but his dragon. Maybe Alastair should tell about Spike now but not while the others were here. He knew he had to tell Uncle George soon but not yet. He needed to look for Spike a little longer. Then he would tell his uncle. When all hope was gone.

"Do you think it's safe to stay here?" Ms. Cassowary asked Uncle George after Mr. Hobson and his group had gone back to check their camp.

"I think so. Whoever came into the camp meant no harm. He could have taken the expensive camcorder and our camping gear. He didn't take anything except the film. I wonder why."

"Do you think it was that creature?"

"The Lizard Man!" Sydney said.

"Possibly," Uncle George said.

"Then you think that was the Lizard Man we saw?" Ms. Cassowary asked.

"One of the things a scientist has to learn is to keep an open mind. My eyes saw and heard the same thing you saw and heard. It looked and sounded like a lizard man. I'll need more proof for my report to the Institute."

How could Uncle George doubt his eyes and ears? Alastair didn't doubt his for a minute. Josh didn't either. His eyes were as big as Mr. Hobson's pith helmet.

Alastair thought his probably were too.

Even Sydney didn't doubt her sharp sneaky little eyes.

Alastair didn't know about Ms. Cassowary. You couldn't always tell with her.

"Time to turn in, sports," Uncle George said.

Alastair and Josh brushed their teeth. They took turns pouring buckets of swamp water over themselves, then soaped up and poured more buckets to rinse themselves.

They probably smelled swampy but they didn't care. All Alastair could think about was his dragon out there in the vast swampy swamp. He didn't know if Spike could swim. The only water Alastair had ever put him in was his weekly bubble bath.

Then a terrible thought struck him. Alastair almost fell down from it. Did Lizard Men eat dragons? Or would that be cannibalism? Was Spike a reptile? Or an amphibian? He didn't know. His head swam with these new questions and doubts and fears.

He hoped Spike was all right. He had his secret weapon. Was that enough in this swamp full of predators? Could he scare off an alligator that had a brain the size of a peanut?

Alastair put on clean shorts and a tee. He filled his backpack and got into his sleeping bag. Josh did the same.

Uncle George stayed by the campfire as it burned down to ashes. He was working on his computer. Alastair wondered what he was typing. Ms. Cassowary sat in a camp chair with her laptop on her knees. The clackety-clack of their keyboards made Alastair sleepy after awhile but he had to stay awake.

At last the keyboards were silent. Where was Uncle George? Alastair squirmed. Josh did the same. Things whirred and clacked and roared and croaked and screeched in

101

the swamp. It was the loudest place Alastair had ever tried to sleep in.

A shadow crossed the tent. Uncle George climbed into his sleeping bag. Soon his snores joined the swamp sounds.

It was time to run away.

Chapter 14

Alastair slid into his sneakers. He shoved his duffle, the one that no longer held his dragon, into his sleeping bag. Even in the dark it didn't look much like him but maybe Uncle George wouldn't notice Alastair was gone if he woke up in the night. Josh seemed to be asleep. Alastair gave him a nudge.

"Wha…" he started to say.

"Shhh. Come on," Alastair whispered. He picked up his backpack.

Josh made a lump in his sleeping bag, too. He already had his sneakers on. They crept out of the tent.

The swamp seethed around them. Didn't it ever sleep? It was noisy in the daytime and noisier at night. Through breaks in the trees a few stars speckled the black sky but they gave no light at all. Alastair took cautious steps, Josh behind him.

A branch snapped under Josh's feet. Alastair stopped. "Be quiet."

"Nobody can hear that with all the screaming and screeching around here," Josh said.

He was right.

They rounded a bend in the trail that led into the heart of the swamp. Alastair took his flashlight out of his backpack. He flashed it on the path. Something white fluttered in the dark. A swamp ghost?

A moth.

"Where are we going?" Josh asked in his normal voice.

"I don't know. We'll just call Spike and hope he'll hear us."

They went deeper into the swamp. The path narrowed. Twice black water gleamed beside them.

"Did you see that?" Josh said.

"What?"

"There in the water. Alligator eyes."

"It was probably a turtle." Alistair hoped it was a turtle.

"It could be an alligator snapping turtle," Josh said.

He would think of that. The dark held many things that might jump out and grab them. Things that might pull them under the black water.

The Lizard Man.

Giant snakes.

Monsters.

Alastair shivered and not with cold.

He had to find Spike. He had to find him in a hurry before something or somebody else did. And before he and Josh got lost in this big swamp.

He imagined the phone call from Uncle George to his mom. "You've lost Alastair in the Green Slime Swamp? Josh too? What am I to tell his parents, that the Lizard Man got both of them? They just disappeared?"

For awhile she would think it was a joke. Then she might cry. He didn't want his mom to cry. Or Josh's parents.

"Come on, hurry up," he said.

"I'm hurrying," Josh said, "but what's the hurry if we don't know where we're going?"

Alastair didn't answer. Deep into the swamp was where they were going on a trail they'd never been on, with things on it that they couldn't see but that could see them. He probed the bushes with the beam of his flashlight.

"Spike!" he called in a loud whisper.

"Spike!" Josh echoed.

No answering zghheeep or mewffff or any of the other Spike words. Just the swamp sounds. The trail got narrower and then it disappeared in bushy growth.

"What do we do now?" Josh said.

Why was he always asking questions?

"How should I know? I've never lost a dragon in a swamp before."

"It's your dragon. You should know how to find him."

"Well I don't. He's never been lost before. I thought he would come back to the camp like he did last night."

"Maybe something got him already."

That seemed more of a possibility when Josh said it than when Alastair thought it. "Don't say that. Nothing's got him. He's just lost. That's all. We can find him."

Spike was such a little dragon. He was probably scared. He had never been lost in a swamp before. Maybe he'd never even been in a swamp. Alastair hadn't either. Nor Josh.

"Spike! Spike! Spike!" Alastair yelled as loud as he could.

No dragon sounds answered.

He found a stick and flailed at the bushes at the end of the path.

Josh did the same, one on the right and one on the left, calling Spike's name louder and louder.

They kept going even though the path had ended

They veered around huge trees with enormous trunks and limbs that twisted like goblin trees in a fairy tale.

Things brushed their faces, the backs of their necks.

It felt like giant hairy spiders!

Alastair yelped. He flashed his light. Spanish moss.

"Spike! Spike! Spike!"

No answer.

They were alone in the dark swamp.

Weren't they?

"I'm hungry," Josh said.

"You're always hungry."

"No, I was full after all that supper. You got anything to eat in your backpack?"

"Just some Spike food. He might be hungry when we find him."

"If we find him."

"Don't say that. We got to find him. Keep looking." Alastair called again. It wasn't working. He started singing.

"Why are you singing? I thought we were supposed to be dragon hunting."

"We are. These are Spike's favorite songs. Maybe he can hear them if he can't hear us shouting." He went on with Old MacDonald had a farm.

"What time is it?"

Alastair looked at his arm. Oh no! He'd forgotten to put his watch back on after the swamp water shower. Now he didn't have the compass that was on it. "I think it's about nine."

"Seems later than that. I'm not usually this hungry at nine."

Alastair knew it was later than nine. The horticulturists had stayed until almost nine. After that they'd cleaned the camp and themselves and it had taken Uncle George a long time to go to sleep. He thought it was closer to ten or eleven. It could even be midnight. They were alone in the Green Slime Swamp that was now all black. The Black Slime Swamp.

Where was the moon when you needed it?

"I think we should go back to camp," Josh said. "Spike could be anywhere. It's a big swamp. Maybe he'll come back on his own."

Josh was right. "We can go back to camp and search in another direction. I can't stop looking until I find him."

"Which way is camp?"

"Back the way we came."

"Which way was that?"

"Easy. Just turn and go the other way."

Josh turned around. He was in the lead now.

He didn't move.

"What's the matter?"

"Everything looks different. I can't tell which way we came after the path ran out."

"I can find the camp. Let me go first." Alastair went around Josh but he didn't know which way they'd come either. They had circled too many trees, gone around too many bushes. "Look for the North Star."

"I can't see any stars. Those clouds are in the way."

"Let's try this way," Alastair said.

Before he took another step his flashlight battery died. He used Josh's but his batteries died a few minutes later. Alastair felt in his backpack but he didn't find anything shaped like a battery.

He didn't think carrot sticks would work.

"Did you hear that?" Josh said.

"What?"

"In those bushes head of us."

The bushes rustled again.

Louder this time.

Something big.

It stood up on his hind legs.

A raccoon?

A wildcat?

A bear?

A cougar?

The Lizard Man?

The thing in the bushes moved toward Alastair and Josh.

Chapter 15

Alastair out-screeched anything in the swamp.

Except Josh.

Josh screeched louder than Alastair.

A voice came out of the dark. "What are you two hollering about?"

"Sydney!" Alastair and Josh said together.

She flashed her light over them as they stood clutching each other.

"What are you doing here?" Alastair had the presence of mind to ask.

"Yeah," Josh said.

"I was following you two. What are you doing out here?"

Why did she always ask so many questions? "We're um…looking for the Lizard Man," Alastair said.

"Oh yeah? Then why are you calling Spike? Who's Spike?"

"We weren't calling Spike," Alastair said.

"No." Josh shook his head.

"We were calling the Lizard Man. Like this. Sppppkt. Sppppkt. That's the sound lizards make," Alastair said.

"They do not. Lizards don't make any sound at all."

"They do," Alastair insisted.

"I've heard them," Josh added.

Sydney didn't believe them but she probably hadn't heard them clearly.

They hoped.

"Maybe she knows the way back to camp," Josh whispered.

"What did you say?"

"Um, he said we're going back to camp now," Alastair said.

"Yeah, it's late," Josh said.

"You can take the lead," Alastair said.

She looked like she was about to say something.

"Since you have a flashlight," Alastair said in a hurry.

"If you know the way," Josh said.

Challenged, Sydney spun around and charged into the blackness following her flashlight beam.

"Good thinking," Alastair said under his breath to Josh.

He didn't know how Sydney could remember the way. Nothing looked familiar to him. They could be in another country.

On another planet.

If another planet had a jungle growing on it.

So far the planets Alastair knew about were all too cold for jungle to grow on them. Or much of anything else.

They didn't find the trail.

And they didn't find the camp.

Finally Alastair said, "Shouldn't we be there by now?"

Sydney stopped. "I was sure it was this way."

She didn't sound sure.

She didn't sound sure at all.

She sounded lost.

As lost as they were.

Spike was lost in the swamp. They were lost in the swamp. And they were lost with Sydney. Things couldn't get much worse.

They could.

And they did.

With the blink of an eye they were in complete darkness again.

"This isn't funny," Alastair said. "Turn the flashlight on."

"I didn't turn it off," Sydney said. "It just went out." She shook the flashlight.

Nothing happened.

"Turn yours on," she told Alastair and Josh.

"Our batteries are dead, too," Alastair said.

"I can't see my hand in front of my face," Josh said.

"Neither can I," Sydney snapped.

Alastair could feel the darkness settling around them. And the things in the darkness.

"Guys, things are out there waiting for their dinner."

"So what," Sydney said, still cross that her flashlight was dead.

"We're the dinner," Alastair said.

The dark felt like thick black velvet. The noise was even thicker. It got louder. And scarier.

"Now what?" Josh asked.

Alastair was all out of answers and jokes and smart remarks.

For once Sydney was out of questions.

"Maybe there's a spare battery in my backpack I missed when I looked before," Alastair said. He rummaged and found the Spike food, the Teagle suit, a comic book, a pair of socks that didn't go in the wash when they were supposed to, a marble.

Why did marbles turn up everywhere?

Alastair bet the astronauts found marbles on the moon. He bet marbles were in outer space.

Marbles were everywhere but in Alastair's backpack.

"Well," Sydney said. "Did you find any?"

"No."

"Now what?" Josh asked the question. Sydney kept quiet for once.

"We should try to follow the North Star," Alastair said.

"No stars tonight," Josh said.

"Well technically there are stars up there," Sydney said. "We just can't see them because of all those clouds."

"That helps a lot," Josh said.

"I think I can feel which way is north," Sydney said. "I have a good sense of direction. I never get lost. Once we were in a cave. The guide asked who knew which way was north. I was the only one that knew."

"Well, you're lost now." Alastair snickered until he remembered it was not a good thing for her to be lost because it meant he and Josh were also lost. "OK, which way is north?"

"This way."

"That's as good a direction as any," Josh said. Alastair gave her his stick to feel around for snakes and things with.

114

He found a shorter one and stuck it in the ground for a marker.

They walked awhile, stopping now and then to look for stars.

Alastair and Josh called, "Spppkt," every few feet.

"Stop that," Sydney said.

"Why?"

"Do you really want to find the Lizard Man in the middle of the swamp?"

Alastair had to admit he didn't. He wanted to find his dragon but he couldn't tell her that. He let Josh go ahead of him and lagged behind a bit to whisper, "Spppkt. Spkkkkt."

Alastair was tired. He felt worse than he ever had in his whole life. He'd lost his dragon. It was all his own fault. He should have left Spike at home where he would've been safe.

He would have been sad with Alastair away but he wouldn't be lost in the swamp.

Why hadn't he thought ahead to the problems of taking care of his dragon on a camping trip?

"It was all Ms. Cassowary's fault for bringing Sydney.

And Sydney's fault for coming.

If Sydney hadn't been along he could have told Uncle George and everything would have been fine.

She came and Alastair had to keep Spike hidden.

If he had asked Uncle George about bringing Spike along, he would have said Sydney was coming with them. Alastair would have left Spike at home where he would be safe. And happy.

Why? Why hadn't he done that? He had to learn not only to think ahead, but to gather information in advance.

The others were getting ahead of him. He hurried to catch up and bumped into a stick. He ran his hand down it.

It was the same stick he'd stuck in the ground. They had just walked in a circle.

"Hey guys, wait up."

Alastair ran after them.

All he saw was darkness.

Where were they?

"Josh? Sydney?"

No reply.

He was alone in the black night of the Green Slime Swamp.

Chapter 16

The buzzing, screeching, whirring, whining, croaking swamp surrounded Alastair. This was the loneliest alone he had ever been in his life. He felt sick. His dragon was lost, his friends were lost, he was lost. This time he was sure things couldn't get worse.

They could.

Things can almost always get worse.

And they did.

Right away.

Alastair couldn't stay in that spot all night. He took a few steps and plunged into black water.

Cold black water.

Cold black water covered with lacy green slime.

He thrashed around. Long slimy stems twined around his legs.

Alastair snorted water up his nose. Something spidery crawled onto his eye.

Things burbled and hissed around him.

Alligators!

Snakes!

Snapping turtles!

Alastair gasped for air and choked on the water. He couldn't get out. Maybe it was quicksand. He had to get out. NOW!

"Help!" he yelled.

Something bellowed in the darkness. Not far away.

Alligator?

"Help!" Alastair yelped a little less loudly. He stopped thrashing.

Something splashed and something bellowed a reply. He was getting out of here.

Fast.

Now.

This nanosecond.

Alastair lunged in the direction he thought he'd fallen from, his arms windmilling until he touched something long and slimy. He leaped in the other direction and felt the bank, silty and slick as a greased playground slide.

He clawed his way up and pulled himself along by vines and other slimy vegetation, making sure nothing could move by itself.

The water wasn't deep.

He was lucky it wasn't quicksand.

He was lucky he hadn't landed on an alligator.

Or a snapping turtle.

Or a snake.

His luck didn't last.

Something green loomed over him.

It was not a tree.

Or a bush.

Something green and glowing.

Glowing green lizard feet stood right in front of him.

Glowing green lizard feet with claws.

Behind them hung a glowing green tail. A scaly glowing green tail.

The Lizard Man.

It had to be.

Alastair gulped. He covered his head and waited to be mauled.

Or eaten.

Whichever came first.

Or whatever a Lizard Man did with his food.

Something touched his hand. It felt like a human hand. A hand patted him on the head. Maybe the Lizard Man was going to pull his head off and eat it first.

The way Claudia popped Gummy bears into her mouth.

He would be a Gummy Alastair.

What kind of teeth did a Lizard Man have?

Fangs?

Grinders?

Serrated like sharks?

He waited.

And waited.

Nothing happened.

Alastair opened his eyes.

The glowing green feet had disappeared.

He raised his head and looked around.

The glowing green thing was gone. He was surrounded by blackness again.

He had been touched by the Lizard Man.

And lived to tell about it. Wait until he told Josh and Sydney. And Uncle George. And Ms. Cassowary.

The Lizard Man is real.

Then he remembered. He was lost in the middle of the black Green Slime Swamp full of alligators, snakes and maybe other Lizard Men.

And even Lizard Women.

The others might not just go away.

Alastair's heart pumped terror through him. He wanted to yell but if he did, something might hear him and come after him.

He wanted to run. He wanted to cry. He wanted his mom. He wanted his dragon.

Alastair felt sorry for himself. Everything had gone wrong. His dragon was lost. He had never felt more miserable and alone in his whole life.

The two most important discoveries of his life and he had botched the first one and couldn't prove the second: finding Spike and seeing the Lizard Man.

Feeling sorry for himself wasn't helping him. He started singing a song he had made up when he and Spike played hide and seek.

"O where O where can my dragon be?

O where O where can he hide?

If I can't find him, will he come home to me?

Or will I search far away and wide?"

The song made him sad. He felt even sorrier for himself. A tear splashed on his knee. It was warm. Warmer than his knee.

What good did it do to sit here in this black swamp night scared and sorry for himself? Whimpering wouldn't get him anywhere. It wouldn't find his dragon. It wouldn't find Josh,

It wouldn't find Sydney either.

He didn't really want to find Sydney but if he found her Josh would probably be with her.

He swiped the back of his hand across his eyes and stood up. He would have to try to find Josh and Sydney. He hoped the Lizard Man didn't get them. What if the Lizard Man had already eaten them and Spike too and that's why he didn't eat Alastair?

He had to find his dragon and his friends—quick if they hadn't already been devoured. Which way to go? Any way was probably the best way as long as it didn't lead back to that cold black water.

He took a step forward. Something bumped his knee. Alastair screeched and leaped two feet off the ground.

"*Zheep*," a tiny voice purred.

Nobody said *zheep* in that voice. Nobody he knew except—

"Spike!"

Zheeeeeeeppppppp, said the tiny voice again.

Alastair knelt in the darkness. Something touched his hand. Something warm and scaly. He opened his arms and Spike climbed into his lap making happy, dragonish noises.

"Oh Spike, I thought I would never see you again. You've been lost two nights and a day. Where have you been little guy?"

Spike made more noises as if he were telling Alastair the story of his adventures in the swamp.

It sounded like he'd had a good time.

"I wish I could speak dragon," Alastair said. "I'm glad you're back now. Please don't run away again. I missed you so much."

Spike butted his head against Alastair's arm.

"Now that I've found you, maybe you can help me find Josh and Sydney," Alastair said.

Zheep zheep, Spike tugged at Alastair's jean leg.

"Oh no. Sydney. I'll have to put the Teagle suit on you. And the leash too because I can't see to follow you in the dark."

Alastair opened his backpack and felt around for the furry parts of the dragon disguise. He tugged it over Spike's head. It was hard dressing his dragon in the dark. He had to do it by feel and hope he got it on straight. He gave Spike the carrot to munch on while he pulled and tugged and adjusted the suit. Then he snapped on the collar with the attached leash.

"OK, fella, lead the way. Find Josh."

Spike swallowed the last bite of his carrot, burped a dragonish burp and sniffed the swampy air.

Alastair sniffed too. All he smelled was—swamp. Spike seemed to smell something else. He trotted off into the bushes with Alastair following.

Spike led him on a curvy route through the dark swamp and soon he heard voices ahead.

"I think it's this way," Josh said.

"No, it's this way," Sydney said.

"Hey, Josh! Sydney!"

The bushes rustled.

"Alastair!"

They grabbed him in a group hug, both talking at once.

"We thought you were lost forever," Josh said.

"We thought you had fallen into the water and been eaten by an alligator," Sydney said.

"Or a python," Josh said.

"Or the Lizard Man," Sydney said.

He almost had been—all of those things but especially by the third one.

"I'm glad we found you," Sydney said.

"I think it was the other way around," Alastair said. "I found you."

"No way," Sydney said. "We weren't lost, you were."

"Excuse me," Alastair said, "but you were lost and guess what—you still are."

Sydney couldn't argue about that. "At least we aren't wet," she said.

"Yeah. What happened to you?" Josh said.

"I um, fell in the water."

"And you lived to tell about it!" Josh said.

"Barely." That wasn't all he had lived to tell about. Alastair wasn't ready to talk about the Lizard Man. Not yet.

"What was that?" Josh said.

"What? I didn't hear anything," Sydney said.

"I felt something," Josh said. "It felt like…well like…" his voice trailed off. He had recognized what he'd felt.

Spike.

Alastair took a deep breath. He would have to explain Spike to Sydney. There was no way around it. She would see him when they got back to camp. The campfire would give off enough of a glow to show that Alastair had a Teagle on a leash leading them to camp.

"Um, Sydney," Alastair began.

Chapter 17

"He's a what?" Sydney's voice shot up.

"Dog, a Teagle dog."

"How did he get here?" Sydney said after she had felt Spike in the dark.

Alastair hoped he'd got all the scales covered up, especially the ones on the tail. She didn't mention scales so he guessed he must have.

"I sneaked him in my duffle bag," Alastair said. "He got loose last night and ran away in the swamp. Josh and I were looking for him."

"I thought you were trying to find the Lizard Man first."

"Are you nuts? We wouldn't go looking for the Lizard Man in the swamp by ourselves at night," Josh said.

"No." Alastair remembered what he had seen. Should he tell them now? He decided to wait until they got back to camp. It would be less scary then. "I would only go in the swamp at night looking for my pet Teagle."

"I bet you're going to be in big trouble," Sydney said. She sounded happy about it.

Alastair thought so too, but it wouldn't be as bad as before he found Spike. He would worry about that later, when they weren't lost in the scariest blackest swamp in the world. First they had to find their camp.

"Let's go back now," Alastair said.

"Does anybody know the way?" Josh asked.

"Get your dog to lead us back," Sydney said. "If he can."

"I'm sure he can," Alastair said. "He found me. Home, Spike."

He kept his worries to himself. Maybe Spike knew the way back to camp, but if he did, why hadn't he come back before now?

A glimmer of moon came up and showed through breaks in the tree canopy. It gave them a little light, not enough to see more than shapes, but it was better than the total blackness before.

Josh and Sydney fell in line behind Alastair as Spike trotted through the swamp, stopping to sniff things from time to time. He seemed to know where he was going as he led them through the dark swamp.

"There's a light up ahead," Alastair said. "Good boy, Spike. Take us home."

"Aunt Rita and Uncle George must have discovered us missing and built a campfire to guide us back," Sydney said.

Alastair didn't think so. It was hard to wake up Uncle George in the middle of the night. He was probably still cutting z's.

"This doesn't seem like the trail from our camp," Josh said. "It's not as twisty."

"Maybe we're on a different path," Alastair said. "It's not like we know where we are."

"Are you sure your dog knows the way back?" Sydney said.

"Of course he does," Josh said. "He's a dog."

Not exactly, Alastair thought but kept his thought to himself. Spike had never tracked anything that Alastair knew about. Except Gruesome. He could probably track Gruesome into outer space. Alastair didn't know if he could track anything else.

"It's a campfire!" Sydney peered around Alastair. "I knew it. Here we are, Aunt Rita."

She ran ahead with Josh right behind her.

Spike stopped and pulled Alastair back.

"Wait, Sydney," he said but she ran ahead into the lighted clearing with Josh right behind her. It was too late to stop them.

Spike tugged the bottom of Alastair's jeans and pulled him behind some bushes. They crouched and watched the clearing as Sydney and Josh reached the fire and turned around looking for something familiar, the tents, the picnic table, the canoe tethered to a tree. Instead of Ms. Cassowary's SUV and Uncle George's van, a panel truck was parked in the clearing.

Two men appeared from the back of the truck where they were loading wooden crates. They walked over to Josh and Sydney. They wore long black beards and looked like the two botanists that had been working so hard in the swamp.

Saved! Alastair had been afraid they were swamp thieves. He started to stand up.

Growwwwwwffff. Spike growled low in his throat.

"What is it, fella? They're just the two botanists we saw working in the swamp."

Grrrruffffff. Spike shook his Teagle-suited head.

Alastair crouched behind the bush and waited to see what Spike was growling about.

"Well, well. Look, Elroy. We have visitors," the taller man said.

"It's those kids we saw in the canoe," the short one said. Elroy.

Their voices sounded familiar. He'd heard them before somewhere. And that name. Alastair tried to remember. Maybe at Mr. Hobson's. He'd heard a lot of names at his neighbor's. It was all right. They were plant scientists. Sort of like Uncle George. They were safe.

Spike wasn't convinced. He recognized their voices, too. He growled a long low grrrrrrr in his throat and kept growling.

Alastair stayed where he was. Always trust your dragon.

"What are you doing?" Sydney demanded.

When they didn't answer, she marched over to one of the crates. "Just as I thought. Plants. You're plantnappers."

"No, indeed, you're mistaken," the taller one said. "We brought these in to plant."

"Yes, indeed," Elroy said. "We're replanting."

"No way! You can't fool me," Sydney said. "Nobody would be planting in the middle of the night. You're plantnappers!"

"You're mistaken," the taller one repeated. "We're just about to plant these. We're taking them to another site."

"Yes, that's what we're doing," Elroy said. "We're replanting."

"You can't fool me," Sydney said.

Why wasn't she thinking? You don't accuse two perpetrators in the black Green Slime Swamp in the middle of the night of committing a crime. Even Alastair could think that far ahead.

Josh grabbed her shirt and pulled her back but it was too late. The plantnappers grabbed them and hustled them into the back of the truck. They locked it and put the last crates into the cab. Elroy kicked a little dirt over the fire and they got in the truck. They were about to drive away with Josh and Sydney in the back.

His friends were being napped along with the plants. Alastair stood up. He had to stop them but how?

The leash jerked him into action as Spike ran into the clearing. Alastair raced behind him.

"Stop, Spike. They'll get you too. We have to find Uncle George."

Spike didn't listen. He faced the truck across the cleaning just as the nappers slammed the truck's doors.

"Come back, Spike. They'll run over you!"

Spike didn't move. Nobody could budge a dragon when he didn't want to be budged.

"All right, Spike. We'll stop them."

Spike's eyes turned purple. He opened his mouth. He puffed up to twice his size. The Teagle suit strained and pulled almost off him.

Alastair stood behind him. This was their only chance to save Josh and Sydney.

Spike puffed up another size. The Teagle suit looked like little handkerchiefs tied on him now. His eyes glowed red. He opened his mouth wider as the taller napper turned the key to start the truck's engine and ground the gears. The lights weren't on yet.

Josh and Sydney pounded on the sides in the truck.

"Let us out!" Josh yelled.

"We'll rip your plants to pieces." Sydney yelled.

The truck engine roared to life. The tires rolled forward toward Spike and Alastair.

"Run, Spike." Alastair yelled.

Spike planted his dragon feet and braced himself. His mouth was wide open now, a cavern with something smoldering deep inside.

He took a deep breath.

Ribbons of red fire shot out into the darkness.

A river of red fire spurted like Fourth of July fireworks.

A torrent of liquid lava rolled toward the truck.

The truck kept coming.

"It's that Teagle!" screamed Elroy. "We're gonna be cremated."

The plantnapper applied the truck's brakes but it was too late.

A giant flame roared across the clearing straight for the truck.

"No, Spike. Not the whole thing," Alastair yelled. "Josh and Sydney are in the back."

He need not have worried. Spike had taken that into account. The long flame divided like a serpent's tongue. The clearing glowed as bright as day, lit by dragon fire as the forked flame engulfed each of the truck's two front tires with a hissing sigh.

The tires melted into puddles of rubber and the front of the truck fell to the wheel rims with a clunk.

Spike opened his mouth again. His eyes boiled like cauldrons of fire. The forked river of fire roared from his throat as the nappers tried to get out of the truck cab.

Spike's eyes blazed. He was four times his normal size now, fire shooting out of his mouth in a great arc of flame.

"No, Spike," Alastair yelled. "Don't incinerate them."

The flames seemed to stop in front of the nappers and hover there. The nappers didn't even try to get away. Their faces locked in terror as they awaited their fate.

133

The fire stopped just short of them, touching on their tips of their black beards and then it was gone.

The nappers looked down at their burning beards.

"Eeyow!" they screeched and ran to the dark lagoon behind the truck. They bent over and doused their beards in the black water.

A pair of red eyes watched them from the water's surface.

"Alligator!" they screamed, backtracking as fast as they could, pulling at the remains of their black beards. Most of the beards came off in their hands. They were fake.

Alastair got a good look at their faces without the beards. Now he knew who they were.

Spike did too. He took a step toward the nappers.

"Run!" Elroy screamed. "It's that dragon dog."

They ran in a circle around the smoldering campfire. They didn't seem to know which way to go with Spike in front of them and the alligator behind them. Spike opened his mouth again.

Elroy turned and ran down a rutted track in the swamp, his accomplice on his heels.

Spike ambled after them.

"No, Spike, let them go," Alastair said.

Spike stopped and looked at him as he watched the plantnappers swallowed by the blackness of the deep swamp. He trotted over to the black lagoon and stood on the bank.

He and the alligator stared at each other for a minute. Spike opened his mouth.

The alligator sank and swam away under the dark water. That alligator didn't want to be incinerated either.

Spike lowered his mouth into the water. Alastair heard a distinct sizzling sound followed by a long aaaaaaahhhhhhh.

Then Spike slurped the water of the Green Slime Swamp.

"Hey—what's happening out there?"

"Let us out of here!"

Josh and Sydney pounded on the sides of the truck.

Alastair hesitated. Spike was slurping away. His eyes didn't glow anymore. And he seemed to be almost back to his normal size. His Teagle suit almost fit him again.

"Help! Help!" Sydney and Josh yelled together.

Spike had settled down to a steady slurping. Alastair went to the back of the truck and unlocked it. Josh and Sydney jumped down.

"What happened?"

"Where are the nappers?"

Sydney looked at the truck. "What happened to the tires?"

Josh looked at Spike. "Why is he drinking all that water? Where's the alligator they were screaming about?"

"What's going on?" Sydney demanded. "What's your dog doing?"

"Can you keep a secret?" Alastair asked Sydney.

"What kind of secret?"

"A big one."

"It depends on what kind of a secret it is."

"You have to promise or I won't tell you."

"Oh, all right. I promise."

"My dog isn't a dog. He's a dragon."

Chapter 18

"A WHAT?"

"A dragon."

"You said he was a Teagle."

Josh snickered but it wasn't funny to Alastair. He sighed. This was going to be a long night. "I know. That's his disguise. The secret is that he's a dragon."

Josh had poked the fire so they could see. Sydney stared at Alastair in the firelight as if he had just said that he, Alastair, was the Lizard Man.

Josh added a handful of sticks to the fire. It flared up dispelling some of the darkness. They sat around it as Alastair and sometimes Josh told her the story of finding Spike in the petunia bed.

When they finished she didn't say anything for awhile. She watched Spike as he slurped away. "When will he stop slurping?" she asked finally.

"I don't know. It took a lot of firepower to melt those tires. And then to singe their fake beards. "

"Does Aunt Rita know about Spike?"

Alastair nodded.

"And Uncle George?"

He nodded again.

"Mr. Hobson?"

"No," Alastair and Josh said.

"I heard him ask about your Teagle dog."

"He thinks that's what Spike is. A Teagle dog," Alastair said.

"Nobody knows but me, Josh, my parents, Uncle George, Ms. Cassowary and the Photon Institute."

"What about the nappers?" Sydney said. "They know."

"They know, but nobody believes them," Alastair said. "They've never seen Spike without his dogsuit on."

"Last fall they pretended to be the president and secretary of the Teagle Society," Josh said.

"The tall one was Ms. Vlondemir and the short one was Mrs. Poppentree."

"Elroy," Josh added. "Mrs. Poppentree's name is Elroy."

"How did they get caught?" Sydney asked.

"Um, Spike incinerated their rainboots," Alastair said.

"They fainted and their wigs fell off," Josh said.

Sydney stared at him. "This is the most exciting thing I've ever heard. A real dragon!"

"You can't tell anybody," Alastair said.

"Not even your parents," Josh said. "Mine don't know either."

"You promised," Alastair reminded her.

"I know. Hasn't that dragon finished slurping yet?"

Alastair went down to the water. Spike lapped steadily. He showed no sign of stopping.

"It's time to go, little guy."

Slurp. Slurp.

"We have water at our camp. All you can drink."

Spike raised his head. Water dribbled from his smiley mouth. A frill of the lacy green duckweed was caught on his teeth. Alastair reached to take it off but Spike chewed it up and swallowed it.

"You like duckweed? I'll have to add that to my notes."

Alastair had a lot to add to his notes after tonight. He had learned a lot of new things about his dragon.

He could track through the dark swamp.

Stare down an alligator.

Recognize voices. Adjust his firepower to fit the situation.

Puff up four times his size.

And be friendly with a Lizard Man.

Alastair would keep that last one to himself for now.

"Let's go back to our camp, fella. You think you can lead us there?"

Spike took one more gulp of water and trotted with Alastair back to the campfire.

Slosh. Slosh.

"Why is he sloshing like that?" Sydney asked.

"I think he slurped the entire Green Slime Swamp," Alastair said.

Spike had shrunk all the way down now and was himself again. His Teagle suit fit him except for the bit around his stomach which was still filled with swamp water.

Sydney stepped back as he took a step toward her.

"He won't hurt you," Alastair said.

"He's a friendly dragon," Josh said. "If you're not a dragonnapper."

"Or Mr. Hobson," Alastair said.

Sydney put her hand out, fingers tucked under and let Spike sniff the back.

He opened his mouth. Sydney didn't flinch. Spike's little dragon tongue came out and gave her hand a lick.

"See, he likes you," Josh said.

He did, to Alastair's amazement.

They doused the campfire and Spike led them back to their camp.

Alastair's stomach sank to his knees as they came in sight of the tents. He wished he could crawl back into his cot and sleep until morning. He could hide Spike, and Uncle George would never know he'd been lost in the swamp or even that he'd brought Spike along on the expedition.

They had to stop the plantnappers.

"Are you going to tell?" Josh asked.

"Got to. We have to report the nappers before they escape."

He and Josh went to their tent while Sydney woke up her aunt.

Uncle George was snoring a little puttputting motorboat snore when Alastair shook his shoulder. "Uncle George?"

The snore stopped briefly then resumed. "Uncle George!" Alastair said in a louder voice.

Nothing happened.

"I'll help," Josh said. Together they shouted, "UNCLE GEORGE!"

Uncle George erupted from his cot. "What? What's happening?"

"Um, Uncle George, I have something to tell you."

Alastair felt Spike against his ankle and thought it could be a lot worse. He could be telling his uncle that he had lost his dragon.

"What time is it?" Uncle George looked around. "Is it still tonight? Or did I sleep through the day and it's tomorrow night?"

"No you didn't. It's still tonight," Alastair said.

Uncle George yawned. "Guys—can't this wait until morning?"

"No, it can't."

"OK, sport." Uncle George got up and put on his clothes while Alastair and Josh went out to wait by the table.

Uncle George joined them in minutes. He didn't seem to notice Spike by Alastair's feet. The dragon seemed to sense that Alastair needed his support.

Josh gathered a few sticks and kindled a bright blaze by the time Ms. Cassowary joined them.

"What's this all about, sport?" Uncle George said.

Ms. Cassowary knew. Alastair could tell by her face. She looked like she was about to laugh. Alastair didn't see what was so funny. Her niece was almost kidnapped.

"Um, I brought Spike along in my duffle bag, Uncle George."

"Spike?" Uncle George looked around and spotted Spike

sitting on his haunches, smiling his little curly smile as he munched a piece of duckweed he'd snagged.

Alastair continued the story, the problems of feeding Spike, dragon latrine, keeping him hidden. "Somehow, Spike got out of my duffle bag. I don't know how. It was zipped up when I found it. He might have got out by himself but I don't know how he rezipped the bag."

As the words left his mouth, Alastair knew. The Lizard Man had let Spike out and zipped the bag up.

He hadn't decided yet what to do about the Lizard Man. One thing at a time. "Josh and I went to look for him and Sydney followed us. We got lost and Spike found me and led me to them. Then he took us to the botanists' camp."

"I knew those beards were fake!" Ms. Cassowary said when Alastair finished the story of their adventures that night.

"We have to get those nappers apprehended," Uncle George said going for his cell phone. He talked to the county police.

"They're on their way," he said, clicking off. "They'll be on the lookout for the nappers. They can't have gone far on foot and from our description of them, nobody would pick them up in the middle of the night."

"Are you um, mad at me?" Alastair asked.

"No not mad. "Bothered you didn't tell me. Concerned that you and your friends and the dragon were in danger. You should have told me as soon as Spike disappeared."

"I thought he would come back like he did before. I thought I could find him and nobody had to know." Alastair's voice ran down. He looked at Spike as he tried to choke back tears.

Spike stood up and climbed into Alastair's lap. He nuzzled Alastair's chin. Alastair's arms folded around the dragon as he began to make a low dragon purring sound.

"You should have told me you'd brought him," Uncle George said.

"I would have, but then things got complicated." Alastair cut his eyes in Sydney's direction.

"I understand, but you have to think ahead when you're responsible for a valuable dragon."

"I did think ahead. I thought he wouldn't eat if I left him home alone for two weeks. I thought I could take care of him." He could have, too if Spike hadn't got loose and run away. If the Lizard Man hadn't let him loose. How could he have thought ahead to that? He would have told Uncle George then if Sydney hadn't been here. Who could have thought ahead to her?

"You won't do this again, will you?"

"No. I promise."

Uncle George smiled. "Something good came out of it. If you hadn't acted as you did, brought Spike along, the plantnappers would have got away with stealing all those crates of rare plants."

"So all's well that ends well," Ms. Cassowary said.

Alastair could have hugged her for that, he realized with a shock.

Hugged Ms Cassowary? Was he out of his mind?

Chapter 19

The camp was up early the next morning. Alastair was glad he didn't have to hide Spike anymore. He took his dragon down to the water's edge for a breakfast of duckweed and swamp water. Spike was still thirsty and slurped up more of the Green Slime Swamp.

Uncle George called Mr. Hobson on his cell phone and told him what had happened leaving out the part about the dragon. As they were finishing a big camp breakfast cooked by Uncle George, the Horticultural Society arrived ready to replant what the nappers had crated up.

"I thought you said you didn't bring that Teagle," Mr. Hobson said. He marched up to Spike. "See here, dog, don't you bother any of these rare plants in the swamp."

Spike looked up at Mr. Hobson as innocently as only a baby blue dragon can look. He opened his smiley dragon mouth and before Alastair could say a word, out came a huge monstrous dragon burp.

Green Slime Swamp water gushed out of Spike and sloshed onto Mr. Hobson's sneakers. His feet had been on dry land but now they were in the middle of a puddle of green swamp water. Green swamp water that was slimy with well-chewed duckweed.

Mr. Hobson leaped back. "Control your dog," he yelled.

"I can't control his burping," Alastair said. "I doubt that he can either."

"That dog must have slurped up most of the Green Slime Swamp," Mr. Hobson said.

If only he knew, Alastair thought.

"He is a menace," Mr. Hobson went on, "he and that dog Gruesome."

Ms. Troutman took out a clean handkerchief and tried to mop up Mr. Hobson's feet. They had a cabbagey, spinachy look.

And smell

Mr. Hobson's face was almost the same color. He looked like he was about to lose his breakfast. He rinsed his feet, sneakers and all in the swamp water, keeping a wary eye out for alligators.

And Teagles.

"He's no menace," Ms. Cassowary came to Spike's defense. "Little dogs can't help it if they have to burp." She gave Spike a leftover camp biscuit almost as big as his head.

"Besides, he helped catch the plantnappers," Sydney said.

"How did he do that?" Dr. Smith asked.

"Um, he led us to their camp," Alastair said. "He's a good tracker."

Alastair worried about how he would explain the melted tires as Spike let them to the napper's camp.

He didn't have to.

"Would you look at that?" Dr. Smith said.

"Those plant nappers parked too close to their campfire. It must have spread and melted their tires," Mr. Goldglass said.

"The wind must have blown the fire onto the tires," Mr. Hobson said.

Alastair stared at the scorch marks on the ground in front of the truck and its tires. The real campfire had been at least ten feet away from the truck. All signs of it had been erased. Nothing was left to show where the truck's tires had been incinerated by Spike.

Somebody had tidied up the crime scene.

It had to be the Lizard Man.

The Society members took the crates out of the truck and opened them. They were filled with all of the swamp's rare plants, orchids, Venus flytraps, and sundews.

"This is why we weren't finding many rare plants," Ms. Watts said. She looked like she had found Captain Kidd's treasure.

"These are some of the rarest plants in the world," Ms. Troutman said. "Look at that parrot orchid."

She pointed to a red and blue orchid with a curved yellow petal that looked like a parrot's beak. Another plant she said was a Cinderella orchid that looked like a glass slipper and another she called chili pepper orchid because that was what it looked like. Rarest of all though, was the orchid called Emerald Alba because it was the color of emeralds at dawn.

"You three have saved the Green Slime Swamp plants from possible extinction," Ms. Watts said.

"It was truly a heroic deed," Ms. Troutman said. "Don't you agree, Leonard? Sydney, Josh and Alastair have been truly heroic."

Mr. Hobson paused while opening a crate.

He did not look happy.

He looked like somebody was about to burp Green Slime Swamp water on him again.

"Leonard?" Ms. Troutman prompted.

"Er, yes, very heroic." He pried up the crate lid with a lot more energy than the job needed. The top flew off and Mr. Hobson toppled over, catching himself as his head went down with the plants.

"Careful, Leonard," Ms. Troutman said. "Did you hurt any of the plants?" She hovered over the crate checking for damage.

Mr. Hobson gave Alistair and Josh a look. It wasn't their fault Ms. Troutman was more worried about the plants than Mr. Hobson's head.

"Where's that Teagle," he growled.

Spike was munching duckweed, watched from afar by the wary alligator. Alastair noted that the gator was out of Spike's firing range.

They all spent the next three days replanting the stolen plants. The horticulturists marked their sites on a grid map of the swamp and took lots of pictures.

Spike helped by digging little holes with his paws for Alastair, Josh and Sydney to plant the sundews in. He seemed to know where to find good places.

Mr. Hobson kept his distance but the other members patted him on the head and said what a wonderful planter dog he was.

Alastair's group kept an eye out for the Lizard Man but nobody saw him, or any signs of him.

On his own, Alastair checked for footprints around the nappers' camp and where they had seen the Lizard Man at their camp. Both sites looked like they had been swept with a brush. Alastair was sure the Lizard Man had tidied up his footprints.

Later, Alastair and Josh rode with Ms. Cassowary and Sydney to Mr. Johnson's store for supplies. They left Spike in Uncle George's care.

Sydney wandered around the store while Alastair and Josh chose cookies for the afternoon break and Ms. Cassowary got the things on her list.

"Pssst." The boys looked up. Sydney motioned to them to come into the back room while Mr. Johnson was ringing up Ms. Cassowary's purchases.

They slipped out of the grocery area. The back room was crowded with fishing supplies, buckets, cleaning things, tools.

"Look." Sydney pushed the door back to show them what was hanging on a hook in the wall. They stared at the limp lizard suit.

"There's the Lizard Man," Sydney said.

"Oh, wow!" Josh said. "The Lizard Man is just a lizard suit."

"You mean Mr. Johnson in a lizard suit," Sydney corrected.

"I know that," Josh said. "You don't think I thought an empty lizard suit was running around in the Green Slime Swamp, do you?"

Sydney shrugged. "You're a boy. Boys don't use much of their brains. Anyway, I found the Lizard Man."

Alastair examined the scaly green costume. "We better go back before Mr. Johnson sees us in here," he said.

Mr. Johnson sent them back to camp with an extra cooler for ice because replanting the napped plants was hot work. A lot hotter than gliding along in the Noire in a canoe.

Sydney could hardly wait until they were in the SUV to tell her aunt of her discovery.

"Good work, Sydney," Ms. Cassowary said.

Alastair bet she would have to write a report.

He bet she would want to write one.

She could hardly wait to tell Uncle George. She burst out of the car before she and Josh had their seatbelts unbuckled.

"I found the Lizard Man!"

"Good work, Sydney," Uncle George said after she finished telling him about the lizard suit. "This is the kind of detective work we do at the Photon Institute."

Alastair was unconvinced by the lizard suit. The Lizard Man he had seen both times had looked more alive than a man dressed up in a lizard suit would look. He had been sure the scales, the claws were all alive and real. And the Lizard Man had sort of glowed. If he'd been Mr. Johnson, would he have left Alastair lost in the swamp? Alastair didn't think so.

Later that day Uncle George got a call from the police. They had picked up the plantnappers. They hauled the perps over in handcuffs to the camp to be identified. "We found them tied to a tree by the road," said the policeman whose name was Clark.

"They were babbling about monsters and alligators. Didn't make good sense," said his partner Beaumont.

The nappers looked addled and afraid. Their hair was tangled, their clothes torn. Remnants of black beard stuck to their chins. When they saw Spike in his Teagle suit as he nibbled a pear, they babbled again.

"That dog is a dragon," the former Ms. Vlondemir said.

"Yes, a real dragon," said Elroy, alias Mrs. Poppentree.

"He looks friendly enough to me," Beaumont said.

"Cute little fella," said Clark scritching Spike's head.

153

Alastair hoped they wouldn't examine Spike closely.

He hoped Spike wouldn't purr.

It would be hard to explain a purring dog.

He didn't.

Spike was a smart dragon.

He knew when to keep quiet.

"Are those the men who tried to kidnap you?" Ms. Cassowary asked, taking attention away from Spike.

"Yes," Sydney said.

"Yes they are," Josh confirmed.

Alastair nodded. "Absolutely."

Uncle George and Ms. Cassowary filled the policemen in on the pair's past history of attempted dognapping in Hilliard.

Chapter 20

Alastair thought the Lizard Man might come back to see how things turned out. He knew who had erased the nappers' campfire and made those scorch marks so it would look like the campfire had spread.

And who had melted the truck's tires.

And who had tied up the nappers.

The real Lizard Man.

Alastair was sure it hadn't been Mr. Johnson in a lizard suit.

He watched for either of them to appear, the real one or the fake one but neither came.

Mr. Hobson however did. Every time Alastair got some distance from the group, Mr. Hobson showed up. He was keeping his eye on Alastair and Josh. And Spike.

Alastair was bothered by Mr. Hobson's constant company. Josh too, but not Spike. He snoozed in the shade, noshing on snacks from the Society's members. Every now and then he sidled up to Mr. Hobson and let out a modest burp.

Every time, Mr. Hobson jumped.

Spike smiled his curly dragon smile and ambled off to munch duckweed.

"It's all right, Leonard. The pup likes you," Ms. Troutman said. She gave Spike little tidbits from her backpack, a handful of raisins, an apple, and a cracker which he accepted politely but later, Alastair found the cracker under a leaf. Spike only like crackers with peanut butter spread on them.

By the time the last of the rare plants had been returned to the wild, Uncle George got a call from the Photon Institute.

"It's time to pack up, sports. We'll have to head back tomorrow. The Institute has some information for me to evaluate. This expedition seems to have proved that the Lizard Man is a hoax. However, until I have seen Mr. Johnson in the suit, I have to leave my conclusion open-ended. I haven't determined why the Lizard Man appeared to us that night. What his purpose was. If it was Mr. Johnson in disguise, he knew why we were there and had no reason to scare us away."

"Does that mean we might come back to the Green Slime Swamp?" Alastair asked.

"I hope that won't be too much of a hardship," Uncle George said seriously.

"All of us?" Josh asked.

Uncle George nodded.

"Wow! You mean I can come back again?" Josh looked like he'd just been given his own amusement park.

"Us too?" Sydney asked.

"The whole expedition," Uncle George said. "We may never find the Lizard Man, but we can't count this expedition a failure. We saved something valuable that belongs in the Green Slime swamp. Who knows what we'll do next time?"

They took a last canoe ride before lashing it to the top of the van. Spike sat in front of Alastair. He wore his Teagle suit in case they ran into Mr. Hobson's group.

They saw Green Swamp animals—fauna, Ms. Cassowary called them—but no Lizard Man.

"What are plants called?" Alastair asked.

"I know, I know," Sydney wiggled her hand in the air.

"OK, Sydney—what?" Ms. Cassowary asked.

"Horti."

"Horti?"

"Horti. You know from horticulture. Horticulture means the study of growing plants. Horti and culture."

"That's an educated guess, Sydney," Ms. Cassowary said trying not to smile. "The term for the plants is flora. Animals are fauna. Horticulture is the practice of garden cultivation."

"I thought Flora was a girl's name," Sydney said.

Alastair and Josh laughed so hard they almost fell out of the canoe. Spike made funny little noises and smiled up at Alastair. He couldn't have understood. He must be happy because Alastair was laughing.

After that when Ms. Cassowary and Uncle George weren't around Josh said, "Sydney look there's a yellow horti over there."

Alastair said, "What's this horti called," Sydney?"

She glared at them until Alastair decided to stop teasing her. Josh stopped too.

Before they packed up the camp the next morning after breakfast, Uncle George said he would expect a report on the expedition from each of them for his files at the Institute. That was OK with Alastair. He wrote reports for the Photon Institute all the time about Spike.

Then Ms. Cassowary said she would expect them to each send her a copy as well. Uncle George didn't mind if Alastair made mistakes but Ms. Cassowary would. That took all the fun out of it.

Josh looked like he was about to protest but the thought of another expedition kept him quiet.

Sydney was delighted. She loved writing reports. She raised her hand.

"Yes, Sydney," Uncle George and Ms. Cassowary said.

"Do you want us to illustrate the reports?"

"That would be helpful," Ms. Cassowary said.

Uncle George agreed.

That gave Alastair an idea. He borrowed Josh's Instacamera. It only had a few pix on it. He put it in the pocket of his shorts as they loaded their gear up and climbed into their vehicles to drive home. This time Spike was on the seat between Alastair and Josh. Except when he climbed into Alastair's lap to look out the window.

"That wasn't so bad now, was it?" Uncle George asked from the front. "Having Sydney and Ms. Cassowary along."

The boys had to admit it wasn't. It had actually been kind of fun. Most of the time.

Uncle George seemed cheerful even though the expedition had officially failed to find the Lizard Man evidence either for or against. And they had found out some things. They had seen the Lizard Man. And they had a possible explanation for him.

They stopped at Mr. Johnson's store long enough for Alastair to run in and return the cooler.

"Just put it in the back room there," Mr. Johnson, busy with a customer, said.

This was his chance. The lizard suit was still hanging on the hook behind the door. Alastair snapped a quick picture of the pale green suit with its stringy tail. Alastair remembered the Lizard Man's tail that night. It hadn't looked like this one. This suit didn't look anything like the Lizard Man he had seen.

He went back through the store. "Bye, Mr. Johnson. See you next summer I hope."

"You boys come back here real soon now," Mr. Johnson said.

Uncle George started the van and drove behind Ms. Cassowary's SUV. Alastair turned for a last look at the store. As he did, the Lizard Man stepped from behind a tree on one side and saluted Alastair. His tail was long and thick with emerald green scales.

Alastair pulled the camera out of his pocket and snapped the shutter as the Lizard main waved at Alastair. When he looked again the Lizard man was gone.

He put the camera back in his pocket. He had used the last of the film. He would get it developed himself and then he would decide what to do about it. The picture would show the Lizard Man waving while Mr. Johnson stood in the doorway of his store talking to another customer. The picture would prove that Ms. Johnson was not wearing the lizard suit.

The Lizard Man was wearing his own skin.

His own lizard skin.

He was real.

Alastair had seen him and now had proof in this picture.

Should he tell Uncle George: Josh? Anybody? Alastair had the feeling that the Lizard Man didn't want to be discovered. He didn't want to be a freak on TV and stuff. Maybe he just wanted to be left alone, free in his swamp.

Maybe the Lizard Man appeared when people were getting too close to him to scare them away.

The Lizard Man must have been watching them the whole time. He knew where to find Alastair in the water that night.

He had been the one reading the Harry Potter book.

Alastair hoped he had finished it.

He knew about Spike, too. He had let Spike out of the duffle. He had tried to comfort Alastair. And he had led Spike to Alastair and kept his secret.

Now the Lizard Man wanted Alastair to keep his secret.

He would. He would only write what the others knew in his reports.

Spike climbed on Alastair's shoulder to look out the back window. Was he looking for the Lizard Man?

"We'll find the Lizard Man next time," Josh said.

"You don't think it's Mr. Johnson?"

"Not for a minute, but I didn't want to spoil Sydney's discovery."

Alastair grinned.

"You saw him, didn't you? The real one I mean," Josh said.

"You can't tell anybody."

"I won't."

"When we come back we'll convince him to let Uncle George talk to him. He's good at keeping secrets too" That would be the right thing to do," Alastair thought.

He wouldn't forget any of his equipment. Next time he would think ahead.

Way ahead.

Next time.

Made in the USA
Coppell, TX
03 January 2023

10222072R00100